Seasons of Grief

Award-Winning Short Stories by Teens

Lune Spark Books, Apex, NC

Publisher: Lune Spark LLC

PO Box 1443, Morrisville, NC, 27560, United States

www.lunespark.com

Young Writers' Resources: www.lunespark.com/youngwriters

Email: books@lunespark.com

Phone: +1 (919) 809-4235

Hardback ISBN 13: 978-1-947960-39-8
Paperback ISBN 13: 978-1-947960-38-1
eBook ISBN 13: 978-1-947960-40-4

Cover art by Alexandra Adams

1. Short stories 2. Anthology 3. Creative writing 4. Young writers

First edition

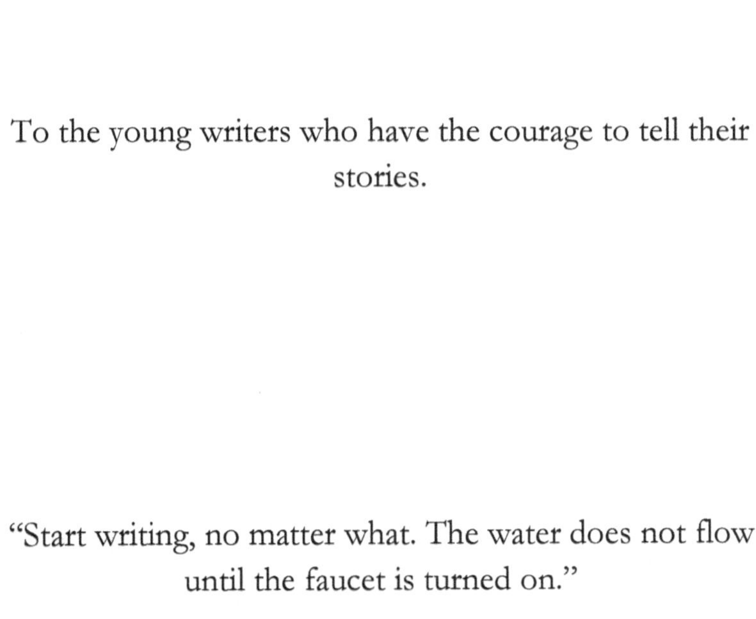

To the young writers who have the courage to tell their stories.

"Start writing, no matter what. The water does not flow until the faucet is turned on."

— Louis L'Amour"

Introduction

When I started the Lune Spark Short Story Contest in 2017, I did not really know what to expect. I had just one goal: to provide a platform for young writers to get discovered and find readers for their stories. I'm very pleased that as of this writing, the contest has entered its fourth year and has acquired a reputation as being one of the best contests in the world for young writers!

I'm also very proud to say that over the past couple of years many of our previous contestants have let me know that this contest worked as a stepping stone toward their goal of becoming a writer. Some of these young writers have successfully released their first novels. So if you know a young writer, please let him/her know about the contest by passing on the website:

lunespark.com/youngwriters

The impact this contest is making in bringing new young writers to the world is becoming more apparent with each year—and that's the biggest reward I can ever expect for all the time I spend every year running this contest.

Just like in past years, the stories this year encompass a tremendous amount of creativity and imagination. I feel proud to introduce yet another excellent anthology of stories by talented young writers.

My special gratitude goes to the following people. Running the contest and publishing this book couldn't have been possible without their help!

- The participants of the 2020 Lune Spark Short Story Contest and their parents for their high degree of engagement, enthusiasm, and support.
- The judges of the 2020 contest: Briana Chen, Jodie Reed, Madeline Worrell, Pankaj Goyal, and Rebecca McNutt. Most of them helped us last year as well—their continued commitment to this cause is highly commendable!

Lastly, the best gift to a writer is a review. So let your take on their stories reach them in the form of a review anywhere you like—on a book website or on your blog. Rest assured that they will very eagerly be reading every single review, looking for encouragement and constructive criticism. Happy reading!

—Pawan Mishra, Apex, North Carolina
January 2021

Contents

Cornflowers

Charlotte Flynn

I have seen the flowers weep. The mist that drizzles over their petals in the blanket of morning, wet dewdrops round and heavy and decorating them with beads of moisture. The saturation of moisture weighs on the petals, dipping their heads toward the ground until the dewdrops fall, the tears dripping onto blades of grass. Their sorrow is so human. I can almost imagine the sadness weighing down on them, how heavy it presses upon their delicate surface, until the flower must shed a tear to be rid of the weight. Their raw emotion is openly expressed in the thin lines on the leaves, dotted with strings of moisture, the entanglement of crisscrossed veins, and the cloud of colors blended into their petals. I once felt connected to them, as if I could lie down and dig my nails into the ground and their coarse roots would reach around my body and slowly absorb my essence.

I used to grow them outside, fields of cornflowers and lilies bowing their gentle heads in light breezes. I used to pluck their delicate heads and weave them into my hair, the dark raven strands starkly contrasting with the light petals. Leon would brush the strays from my eyes, his cheeks caving in as he smiled, the cornflower blue reflected in his irises. My world was painted in cornflower blue, the color of his eyes, the color of our wedding, and the color of the roof over our heads. It was the color I tasted when I felt our child growing inside me, a delicate connection I clung to because she was a part of me. I was sheltering a new life; I could feel it grow. I had been a flower; I had known how it felt, to shelter something so beautiful and fragile within me, a bud blossoming. When she emerged, her body was rosy, but she had Leon's eyes. I grasped her tiny fingers and clutched her to my chest, feeling the life radiating from her. She was bright with it, warm energy rolling off her in small waves, sparkling in her eyes. We named her Mila because she was a miracle that fulfilled our lives.

Leon had taken me dancing, the two of us swaying in the fields, the breeze tossing my hair. I had looked into his handsome face, kissed his full lips, and watched as his cheeks and chin dimpled as he smiled. The ghost of his touch lingers, the pressure I had felt on my hips and the curve of my waist. I remember the coarse pads of his palms and how his long lashes made stripes of shadows on his cheeks. I remember the warm nights where he would climb into bed and reach over to me, pressing his chest into mine and sliding his hands to my lower back. He had worked so hard for our family, laboring long days in the lumber industry, his light hair slick with sweat. I had been in the secure bubble of our life; our little house and our child was all I needed.

I remember the day he came home, his face grim. He collapsed into a chair, rubbing his face, his elbows pressed into his knees. The white slip of paper was clutched tightly in his hand, and my eyes darted nervously to it. He had been drafted into the war, and a part of me died inside, the bubble shattered. I had listened to the radio, images of blood and destruction thrown into my mind. His cornflower-blue eyes would be stained from death and darkness, his mind and heart wounded from bloodshed. I clasped our daughter to my chest, fearful of how she would be affected, the future an unknown presence. He pressed his face into my shoulder, sliding his fingers between mine so our palms were touching. The shards of glass in my heart poked at my ribs and jabbed my lungs, my breath rattled. He slipped his wedding ring from his finger, pressing it into my hand for me to protect, promising to return and restore peace to our family. I had stood on the porch waving goodbye, the last time I ever saw him, dressed in his combat uniform and turning toward me to wave back.

The radio became my solace where I sat fervently listening to the gritty voices. I listened to reports of lightning warfare raining from the sky over powerful countries, thunder booming overhead and drowning the cities in sorrow. Sharp pains in my belly stabbed at my insides. I felt exposed, openly vulnerable, and it made me shiver in constant fear and agitation. My fingers clutched at Leon's wedding ring strung around my neck on a silver cord. The cornflower-blue world that once painted the walls of my house molded into a crimson, the tainted color of blood. It was the color of our flag, the black swastika a cruel stain upon the cloth. There was nothing human about them. I had watched tears drip from the flowers with more emotion than any of them. I knew Leon was fighting for them, and that was what we were supposed to support, but the struggle had lasted so long, almost a decade, it was impossible to imagine a world without it in the distance. Mila had grown up with it on the horizon, her childlike wonder unaccustomed to anything else. I lived in fear every day, afraid war would tear our life apart. I pulled Mila close, the pearl of her innocence preserved under my wing and careful watch.

Letters from Leon were shorter, and an ache wore away at my heart during the months he was gone. Losing seemed inevitable. I was torn, wishing for a victory but fearful of what it would bring, hoping for a loss but worrying how we would be punished. I could only think of Leon, praying that God would deliver him back to me. I could see the memory of Leon's face fading from Mila's mind. The pains in my stomach grew stronger and more frequent.

I turned on the radio one day, and images flashed across my eyes as reports shouted the devastation of the Allies, a decisive victory in Normandy delivered to Germany, a twisted turn of fate. The Allies had gambled on the weather, storms lurking menacingly on the horizon, a fatal mistake. Celebrations were heard in the streets, and I plastered a face of joy on the surface, hailing as flags were marched by. The victory was swiftly followed by another in the Battle of the Bulge; unable to seize the beaches of Normandy, Allied troops collected in Antwerp, storming past Holland into German territory and meeting heavy resistance. The victory split the aims of the Allied powers, allowing Germany to recapture the port of Antwerp. Our country demanded a peace treaty, calling for Allied leaders; it seemed as if the world stood on the brink of the finale of war. Rejoicing chorused in the streets, but I saw Death hanging overhead, his long arms grazing the rooftops and swooping to collect unfortunate souls. He soared above the death camps, catching the souls of thousands that perished in the gas chambers. The gold stars patched onto clothing slowly diminished, Jewish families disappearing without a trace. Brightly colored posters and bold words had leaped out at me, instilling prejudice and resentment for these people, but a quiet sympathy stirred within my heart, a sadness I could not quell.

I remember the sharp crack of the nail hammered into my door, hanging a piece of white parchment from it. My fingers trembled as I tore it from the metal, my eyes bouncing across the black words. Leon had fought in Belgium, perishing on the battlefield from a gunshot to the heart. Something broke inside me, and I shrank to the floor, my body raking with sobs. I looked through streaming tears at Mila, just beginning to stand, the memory of her father a blurry ink blot. I looked at his ring strung around my neck, cursing Leon for breaking his promise, begging Leon to return to me. The bubble of our world was gone. We would never dance again.

Mila was growing, her honey-colored ringlets and cornflower eyes reflecting her absent father. I began to vomit, the sharp ache in my stomach manifesting itself because of my anguish. I soon discovered that it was not just anguish, but Leon's second child growing inside me. My fears intensified, heartbroken that my son would not be fathered the way I had hoped he would be. My belly swelled, a second life sheltered in my womb, and my hands wrapped around it with the worry of raising two children in a war-torn world.

I remember the fateful day I turned the knob of the tarnished radio to hear stifled shrieks of glee; Truman had fallen mysteriously ill during negotiations of the peace treaty, replaced by Barkley who's relatively unknown status rendered him ineffective. That loss crippled America severely, weakening the Allies. Rumors of their atom bomb quickly fizzled, leaving an open target for Japan. Churchill was voted out of office from conservative weakness, leaving Britain in disarray. News of their submission shortly followed, German streets erupting in howling madness. I hailed the passing flags with resignation, in a state of subdued shock. When I entered my house, I quietly sobbed. Their symbol of hate had triumphed.

Then I looked at Mila. Her tiny frame against the wooden bars of the crib. In her eyes I saw a future, and a glimmer of hope traced my heart. She was the future. My unborn child was the future. I would raise my children so they would never be like them. I knew Leon was watching us from above. One day, they will find an end to their plague of horror. One day.

One Wish

Sivaranjani Velmurugan

Everywhere I looked, I only saw closed signs tacked to store windows. No gleaming window displays or chattering flocks of shoppers. The few people in sight were wearing the required masks or makeshift face coverings. This place used to be swarming with shoppers, but the coronavirus outbreak has left it empty. I reached up to secure my own face mask before walking toward the only art supply store that was open.

I stepped inside and wasn't surprised by the lack of people. I knew the reason. *Coronavirus.* As I stood there, wondering how long it would take for things to finally return to normal, an impact from behind sent me crashing to the floor. Dazed, I rolled over and realized that a woman had rammed into me with a shopping cart. *Uh-oh.* She grasped my arms and pulled me up. Instinctively, I lowered my head and tried to let my hair fall over my face, but it was too late. She had already seen me. I couldn't decipher her expression, but I assumed that her mouth had dropped open in shock behind her mask. I waited for her eyebrows to pull together in a frown. I waited for her to stare at me with disgust. I waited for her to avert her eyes. Instead, she took a few steps back and said, "I've never seen such gorgeous hair! And striking blue eyes! You're such a beautiful young lady!" At first, I was shocked. And then, I realized something. *My mask. My mask is hiding it. She can't see anything under my eyes.*

For a moment, I was overjoyed. No one had ever genuinely said something nice about my appearance before. My heart swelled with pride. This woman was talking to me like I was normal. She had actually admired my hair and my eyes. These were things that no one had ever noticed about me before. "Are you hurt?" The woman's voice jolted me back to my senses.

"I'm fine. Thanks for helping me up."

As I continued down the aisle, I came across a mother pushing a shopping cart with two toddlers riding in it. The adorable twin children giggled and waved at me with their chubby hands as the mother walked by. Astonished by this gesture, I waved back. I could still hear their laughter as their mother pushed the cart into another aisle. Afterward, I couldn't help but wonder if I had imagined the whole thing. I was used to children crying or screaming when they saw me, but never before had I made any child laugh.

Twenty minutes later, I cheerfully walked out of the art store with a wooden craft plank, a paint set, and a rope in my shopping bag. *From now on, I can just waltz into any store and no one will even glance at me. As long as this mask covers my face, I don't have to be constantly running and hiding and hoping that no one will see me. I can finally be free of the eyes that follow me wherever I go.* Usually, I would have lowered my head and rushed to the car, hoping that no one would notice me. This time, I pushed my hair out of my face and straightened up, beaming as I waved to a passerby. Once I was inside my car and no longer in contact with any people, I pulled off my face mask and rolled down the windows to get some fresh air.

That's when I caught a glimpse of my own reflection in the side-view mirror. A large four-inch birthmark completely covers my lower left cheek in sharp contrast to my fair skin. It's called a nevus. I have a facial giant congenital melanocytic nevus. From force of habit, I readjusted my hair to cover the hairy, slightly raised, dark brown patch of skin under my left eye. When I was younger, the doctors had informed us of a risk that the surgical procedure that was required to remove the nevus might leave severe scars on my face. I ended up never having surgery because I was afraid that it would leave my face even more marred than it already was. That fear still lingers with me.

I continued examining my reflection in the side-view mirror. *Suddenly, I'm in front of the mirror in the girls' restroom, staring at my awful reflection. Kids sneering at me in the classroom. Laughter echoing behind me as I run. Hiding in a dark hallway, tears streaming down my cheeks. Alone at the lunch table. Everyone pointing at me and whispering.*

"It's that ugly girl who's always by herself..."

Shuddering, I pushed the bad memories to the back of my mind. School was a nightmare. The only thing that made it somewhat bearable was my older sister Andrea. "Don't listen to them," she would say. "They don't know what a great person you are inside." When I was younger, Andrea had always been the one looking out for me. She was the one who wiped my tears away and ordered me to be strong. Andrea means *everything* to me. A wooden craft plank. A paint set. A rope. Even the materials that I've bought today are for the special gift that I'm making for her. She's visiting tomorrow, and I can barely contain my excitement!

As I started driving, I remembered my last trip to the same art store, before the coronavirus outbreak...

Heads turned in my direction, and mouths dropped open in shock as I dashed through the aisle. People paused to stare at me and craned their necks to catch a second glimpse of my face. My cheeks burned red in embarrassment. I dropped my head and tried in vain to hide my face with my hair. I wanted to scream and tell them not to watch me. Instead, I forced down my panic and stopped running. If they weren't gaping in disgust at that *thing* on my face, then they might have noticed the way my chocolate-brown hair tumbles down my shoulders in neat layers. They might have noticed my soft, rounded eyebrows or long thick lashes that frame my crystal-blue eyes. They might have noticed my perfectly chiseled nose or my full cherry-red lips. My *one wish* is to be beautiful...

Coming out of the memory, I stopped at a red traffic light.

That day, I remember thinking that my one wish could never be granted. But today showed me that I was wrong. Today, no one frowned or stared. For the first time, they looked at me as an ordinary person. That woman had actually complimented me on my appearance. Before, I was always that girl with the ugly birthmark. Now, I can be beautiful. Somehow, in this twisted world, I've found what I've wanted all along. And it's all because of the coronavirus. The burden that I've carried for my entire life has suddenly been lifted off my shoulders. The sound of a car horn jolted me out of my thoughts. I looked up and realized that the traffic light was already green. Silently scolding myself for zoning out, I started driving again.

I knew it was wrong, but I found myself enjoying this coronavirus situation. It has granted my *one wish.* As I pulled up next to my house, I noticed that my sister's car was already parked in our driveway, even though she was supposed to come home tomorrow. I eagerly bounded up the doorsteps and through the open door. When I stepped inside, the sound of sobbing greeted my ears. I stopped dead. *Andrea.* The shopping bag fell from my hand, spilling all the materials onto the floor. Forgetting everything else, I raced up the stairs and burst into the bedroom. Andrea was sprawled on the bed, crying.

"What's wrong?" I asked, alarmed. My sister looked up at me with reddened eyes.

"I shut down my restaurant today. We couldn't make enough profit cause we didn't get any customers for the past two months. My business…everything that I've worked for my entire life…collapsed." She burst into tears.

I was horrified. Opening a restaurant had been Andrea's childhood dream that she *finally* fulfilled last year. Since then, she'd moved out of town and has been running her business smoothly. But now….

"How did this happen?" I asked. What she told me next

knocked the air out of me like a blow to the chest.

"*Coronavirus.*" She spit out the word with so much hate and anger that I recoiled. "We've tried to assure our customers that we prepare food safely in our restaurant, but they weren't convinced."

"Andrea, I'm so sorry…"

"It's not only my restaurant. Many eateries are going out of business now. They won't be opening anytime soon. I've poured my whole life into my restaurant, and now it's gone. My career is ruined."

I wrapped my arms around her as she wept into her hands. Guilt bubbled up inside me. How could I have been so immature? How could I have wished, even for a second, for the coronavirus to continue? How could I have taken pleasure in the same thing that had shattered Andrea's dreams? How could I possibly care about something as trivial as my appearance when my heartbroken sister was sitting here, crying? How many other people out there have been left devastated by the coronavirus?

I ripped off the mask that I had forgotten to remove earlier and threw it in the trash. Silently vowing to myself to *never* bother about my face *ever* again, I returned to Andrea's side and squeezed her hand. A wooden craft plank. A paint set. A rope. It looks like I won't be making a door sign for my sister's restaurant anymore. The mask has granted my one wish, but at a terrible cost.

White Sails (1832)

WP Dorian

The Thief:

The sharp tang of the Parisian dusk whistles through my hair. My feet thunder against slick cobbles as I pick a sugar merchant's pocket. I run on rooftops, and the blue wind echoes against my cheeks. This city is mine to conquer.

The slow butcher (from whom I stole a cut of prized Normandy steak) chases me through the city streets. I slink from Les Halles and weave along the Seine, disguised in the evening crowds. The butcher stumbles as I run swiftly around sudden corners. On the Rue d'Ormesson, his lumbering feet catch an urchin boy's outstretched cane. The butcher's jaw cracks against the paving stones. His scar will make an ugly sight, but he'll live. This is his warning. The urchin, Souris Rouge, salutes me with a toothless grin and a call of my name. I throw him a penny for his trouble, and he raises the cane in triumph.

"*À plus tard,* Elancé!"

"*Être bien, mon ami!*"

The nighttime breeze and stench of the Seine bristle in my chest, a not unwelcome burn. My throat scratches with exertion, and I quiet my breath, rambling slowly to my lodgings. The dim streetlamps echo against wet streets. I fiddle with my patched sleeves. The lights gleam against the Seine, crowds of learned men and proper ladies taking evening strolls. How it must be to live in comfort like them, free to carve the world. I brush the thought, and dust, and debris, from my coat.

That life is not for me. I knock twice on my door and turn the handle.

The foyer is empty, no bustling meetings or enthusiastic schoolboys—there are always students in our apartments. Ophelia says our home is the center of the political underground in Paris. I laugh, but I do not question it. Her gossip runs through networks best left undisturbed. Ophelia calls from upstairs, and her footsteps crack against the fractured stairwell. My owl-eyed sister, my younger by two years, twelve last month.

"Martial, dinner's prepared, come up," she says.

"Did you use the meat I bought?"

"The meat you stole." Her fingers twitch around the bannister. "I did, but you'd better not find more trouble. Things are hard as they are."

"Does Ethan know?" I follow Ophelia to our door. The floorboards creak, the hinges rustle—home's thin voice.

"*Mon frère*," she begins. "Ethan—" A pause. "Believes in too much and knows too little." She squeezes my shoulder. Her hand is so warm it stings. "He need not know. You procured this meat entirely legally, *oui?*"

I think of the butcher and his cracked mouth, of Souris *Rouge* and his sly cane. The blood against the pavement like raining silver. I look at Ophelia and nod. She opens the door.

I hang up my coat, and Ethan wraps me in a tight embrace. He is kind, literate but unpretentious, with a quiet wisdom. Too young to be our father and too old to be our brother. He took us in from the street, and we've lived with him since. He serves stew at dinner tonight. I set the bowls. Ophelia fetches the spoons. We chat in comfortable but slow spurts.

"Will you permit me a question?" Ethan asks. He wipes his mouth with his sleeve. Ophelia nods. He continues. "Have you heard what they speak of at the café?"

"For the fifth this June?" Ophelia asks.

"Yes." He turns to me. "You know too?"

In the dim candlelight, a foreign danger lights in his eyes.

"I've heard." I swallow. "The insurgents, the rebellion—your friends, your plans, no?"

"They are." He casts his eyes away. "I must keep you safe." He clutches our hands. "But I have a duty to Patria. I must do my part so you may enjoy a better future." He leans forward. "I refuse to serve a society that longs to see us suffer. England, Holland, France—they are all the same—happy to maim and subjugate for their illusions; righteousness, civilization, permanence. I will not be choked beneath their heels. If there is a path to a kinder France, where we outcasts may thrive, I will never cease to pave it. During the insurgence, no matter what becomes of me, know this."

Silence falls like a veil. Ophelia averts her eyes. I stare at my stew.

"I only hope no one is hurt," she murmurs.

"Treason is treason, even for a just cause." Ethan worries his lip and adds softly, "There'll be casualties."

Ethan looks to me. He expects more, but I have said all I am willing to say. His business frightens me, but they are his matters. If he should perish, I know he fought for us. I will take his place, mold myself into the little man I should be, care for Ophelia. If I were older, I should fight with him. If I were stronger, I should stand as his brother-in-arms. If I were honest, I should tell him how afraid I am. For all my tricks, I have none against the scythe, the strike that makes equals of us all. I only hope, beneath the smoke and solitude, he emerges victorious, crowning the dawn with sunlit laurels, the sailor at the helm of a blackened fleet, flying white sails.

***

The Insurgent:

Darkness swaddles the room in languid hushes and husky starlight when Jacob's fist falls hard against the rattling desk. He screams at me, screams my name: *Ethan, Ethan, Ethan!* Over and over, tumbling from his lips like black waters in lowland streams (or like blood, gurgling from his lips like a fountainhead).

"You'll wake the children," I hiss, and clutch his lapel. I try to ignore the fabric slipping through my fingers, like smoke, like wax. "Tell me your fatal plans elsewhere."

"Do what is right." His words ramble on a driftwood tide, and his brow furrows under the thin lamplight. "Join the vanguard."

His fingers pet the torn edge of a pamphlet. Slowly, he says, "You've made the flyers, rallied the crowds." His eyes sharpen. "Who's to say you cannot build the barricade, join the fight—" He falters. He shudders along with the quivering breeze, and he looks at me. "I did not want to do this, to ask this. Julian, he knows you are—"

"Knows I am what?" A roiling, cold dread rumbles in my chest. Subtler yet, but still strong, like a dragging undertow, *rage*, sprouting to the sun in the same stalk as sorrow, or as passion.

"Unattached." The word strikes like flint against his teeth, his iron gums.

I am at the edge of a bloody meadow, where the sod dribbles across the forest's end, and the plough pummels the earth softly in vain. I swallow.

"What you and I have known transcends these rooms, this city, this country. You have run with me, from England, Holland, now France. From gallows, from yokes, from fetid halls overgrown with aristocracy." The lulling tide in my chest draws me to sea. Carried to the depths on the flood tide. "But the children are to me *more*. More than our futile liaison. What I know with them—belonging, fatherhood—it transcends this moment, this day, this life. It is more than you. It is more than this fleeting second in history,"

Jacob sniffs, and for a moment, I fear I have wounded him. But he lifts his head, and it strikes me again—how strong he is, how stubborn. He approaches me, careful to avoid the loudest floorboards, and I await his strike. But his hand falls, like a limp swallow, to his side, and he nods.

"You make a fair point. And foolish as I am, I know you will not be swayed." He holds out his hand, and I offer mine. His calluses sting against mine, and he clasps our hands together. "My friend, we will continue this at my lodgings. I fear when sentiment overtakes us, we are too prone to violence and rage."

We leave the apartment in the thick of night, city air lapping at our skin. Before I follow Jacob into the coming storm, I cast a glance toward the closed bedchamber doors. The children are sleeping. But when morning comes, I will have been a memory, like ghostly plains. When the sun shatters the warmth of night, I will have returned to them, like a ship tossed along the shore, flying white sails.

***

The Daughter:

I wake while Martial wastes in sleep. I bare my face to the dawning city—fresh bread, whining horses. Ethan has not returned, but this is not a new routine. He will knock on the door soon enough and tell us how he's missed us. He'll bring us to the markets, buy us new trinkets, and apologize.

I imagine: Martial shuffles into the kitchen and plucks the dirty pitcher from the cupboard. We drink boiled water side by side in silence as the morning arrives. Ethan bursts through the door in light and a thousand furies and takes us in his arms. His hair will be mussed, his voice raw, but he clutches our backs and maps the grooves in our shoulders. The sunlight catches on his dark eyes, and I resist clinging to his arms and calling him papa, my papa, the first I ever had. He promises: "I will see us through this." The morning filters through the windows, and the vendors clamor their goods. I will be at home.

But hours later, when the sky grays and the first grapeshots have struck the walls, I set the table for two, and imagine him, my found father, proud of his clever daughter. As the horizon dusks and the barricades rise, I imagine he is sailing, sailing on a boiling sea, battle weary and voyage stricken, at the helm of a battered ship, returning home, to me, flying white sails.

Annabelle

Olivia Stevens

You remember the last summer with Annabelle. It was the summer of Popsicle stains, scraped knees, muddy shorts, and firefly nights. It was the last time you truly felt happy.

You remember your euphoria the first day at seeing Annabelle again. You remember kicking your suitcase haphazardly into her room so you could play in the woods with her. You stayed there for hours, slaying invisible dragons to protect your forest castle.

You remember being called in for supper because it was past five o'clock and you'd had a long drive to Annabelle's house. You ate burritos, piling on the sour cream as if it would save your life.

You remember pulling out the trundle bed later and snuggling up against the homemade quilt, the one with the blue star pattern you always slept with.

You remember waking up hours later to Annabelle shaking your shoulder and whispering, *"Come on, or you'll miss it!"*

You remember sneaking out of the house to look at the stars. You stayed outside for a long time, finding constellations and connecting the stars yourselves.

Then, at two o'clock, you snuck back inside and tucked yourselves in just the way Aunt Heather had, so she wouldn't catch you.

You fell asleep immediately, exhausted. Your dreams were filled with wonder.

If only you could return.

But it takes a miracle to undo the past, and Aunt Heather always said, *"What's done is done, and you can't change that, honey."*

If only you could.

You remember waking up at precisely six forty-six to the sunrise. Annabelle was already awake. You were up early enough to watch the sunrise, even though your eyes were drooping. Annabelle had to remind you to stay awake every few minutes so you wouldn't miss the magic.

It truly was one of the most graceful sunrises you had ever seen—the sky brushed with hints of promise as the pale light seeped over the house, over the lake, over the world.

Before you knew it, Aunt Heather was opening the door and telling you to come down for breakfast.

You and Annabelle smiled your thanks as you headed over to Annabelle's closet to pick out an outfit for her. You loved choosing her clothes, and Annabelle loved letting you do it.

You and Annabelle made it downstairs and were treated to the most wonderful French toast in the world. Annabelle let you pick first, and you chose the best piece.

Now you wonder if you should've let her pick first.

Annabelle would always let you have the first choice, and she would accept whatever was left. You remember asking her why one time, and she just said, *"I want you to be happy. If you're happy, then I'm satisfied."*

Looking back, you wonder if Annabelle was an angel trapped inside the body of a nine-year-old.

You need an angel in your life now. But undoing the past is hard, and Annabelle wouldn't want you to change anything.

She always said you were the loveliest person she'd ever known…

You sigh.

It wasn't supposed to turn out this way.

But somehow, someway, remembering Annabelle makes you feel a little bit better. Maybe you're giving her the respect she always deserved.

You remember leaving Annabelle's room. You and Annabelle skipped down the stairs, laughing for no apparent reason. That day was probably the best day of your life.

You remember picnicking with Annabelle and Aunt Heather. You picked raspberries to put into your lemonade but spilt most of it on your sandwich halfway through the meal.

You remember when Annabelle gave you her sandwich to compensate for your loss.

You remember feeling worse about it at that moment, but Annabelle said she never liked peanut butter and jelly. Deep down, you both knew it was her favorite.

But you couldn't argue because Annabelle was always that way—she let you have the best without thinking twice.

Why did she leave? Why did you *stay*?

But you can't undo the past. You can't fix anything.

Lying here, on your bed, with the paint on the ceiling smiling tenderly down at you, you cry.

Why? Why Annabelle? Why was it her? She didn't deserve to die.

You know you shouldn't be sad. Your life is supposed to be perfection at its best. Worry isn't even on the horizon, let alone fear, anxiety, stress…

But now, with everything that's happened in the past week, you let yourself collapse.

Why?

You remember when Annabelle asked Aunt Heather if you and she could play in the woods together. You were overjoyed when Aunt Heather said yes.

You scaled at least seven trees that afternoon, and when you were too exhausted to climb, you waded in the creek, laughing and splashing each other.

You stayed up late again, just you and Annabelle, standing on the back porch. You talked for hours.

When you remember everything Annabelle did for you, you realized she could've been an angel.

Maybe it was right for her to leave.

You remember gazing up at the stars for ages, and even though Aunt Heather knew you were still awake, she didn't come outside to interrupt.

Somehow, you both knew that if anybody talked, it would ruin the peace of the moment. You just stayed silent, appreciating each other's presence.

If only you could feel that way now.

You remember waking up early enough to watch the last of the sunrise. Then Annabelle got out of bed, so you squished yourselves into the same chair to read a book together.

You don't entirely remember the book, but it reminded you of every summer with Annabelle—your late nights stargazing and early mornings outside.

You remember the Fourth of July parade was in the afternoon, and Aunt Heather let you and Annabelle ride your bikes with all the other kids in their tiny Missouri town.

You remember spending the day outside with Annabelle. You got your faces painted the same way, with a little American flag on your right cheek.

You both ate red, white, and blue Popsicles together, then got soaked to the bone when you were playing in her yard with the sprinklers.

But the magic wasn't over yet.

As soon as it got dark, Aunt Heather took out her red-and-white-checkered picnic blanket, the one just the right size for three people and some ice cream.

She took the tub of vanilla ice cream out of the deep freeze, the ice cream she was saving for you and Annabelle. Annabelle got the bowls and spoons.

You took the blanket to the front yard, right by the street, and laid it out neatly. Then Annabelle opened the front door, carrying the bowls and spoons. You set them down on the blanket, staring at the sky with anticipation.

A few minutes later, Aunt Heather came outside with the tub of ice cream.

It was nine o'clock when the fireworks started.

They lasted for hours on end, and every burst of light shone for miles over Annabelle's house. They were shining gems in the sky—soaring sapphires, radiant rubies, dazzling diamonds.

It was past eleven when you went inside.

You distinctly remember that the night of the Fourth was the last time you felt joy. It was July fifth that took your life and flipped it upside down, chortling indignantly all the while.

The morning dawned with a red, angry sky. You remember gaping at the furious sunrise, knowing Annabelle would love to be there—the reds and oranges and yellows blending into one giant canvas of rage.

You didn't wake her. She was still asleep, resting as she had just fallen from heaven onto a cloud.

You stayed there, in front of the window, for ages. Annabelle woke a bit later and asked for you to tell the story of the sunrise. You described it to her as if you had painted it yourself, so she didn't have a choice but to feel awe as you blended the colors with your voice.

You remember the rest of the day, too. You just don't want to.

It was supposed to be a spectacular day. When you remember, it was anything but that.

You and Annabelle were going swimming together. Aunt Heather let you swim alone—mistake number one.

Now that you think of it, maybe the whole day was full of mistakes. Was it a mistake for you to go to Annabelle's at all?

You don't want to remember what happened. It aches too much.

There was a splash. Annabelle was under the water, and you were screaming. And nobody came.

She was gone.

Forever.

You didn't attend the funeral. It wouldn't be right. You just stayed inside, packing your bag and grieving silently, heartbroken.

You blamed yourself for her death.

Later, Aunt Heather would write you a letter and tell you that it was a glorious day, Annabelle's favorite kind. You hated her for doing that. Why must *everyone* remind you of her?

Annabelle didn't deserve to die. She was your angel. *Yours.*

Here you are, though. Sitting on your bed at four thirty-seven a.m., wishing Annabelle is here to comfort you in her Annabelle way.

You feel lost.

You stand up and move to the window. The sun is glimpsing over the horizon, playing peek-a-boo with its radiant face.

You want Annabelle by your side again.

You want to see the world through her eyes.

But maybe—just maybe—if you could hold on to the pieces of Annabelle inside of you, you could be nine years old again.

Maybe.

Just maybe.

Fight

Soumya Shenoy

I wake to the ringing of bells. Gone are the pleasant dreams of being a respected man in the emperor's senate. Reality comes rushing back to me—it's fight day. Today, Roman citizens will flock to the Colosseum by the thousands to see us gladiators fight bloody battles. I'm lucky that I haven't been chosen to fight today. Instead Cassius, one of my fellow gladiators, will be pitted against some poor convict probably caught stealing from the market stalls. It is an execution, glorified for the entertainment of the citizens of Rome. I quickly dress in my armor, a combination of metal plates and animal pelts. I look like a barbarian from the Gaulish lands at the border of the empire.

Cassius and his opponent step into the arena. I compare the two, side by side, and frown. His opponent doesn't stand a chance. Cassius is a head taller than his opponent, built like a stack of bricks, whereas his opponent looks like he hasn't eaten in days. The game starts, and the audience cheers in anticipation. They know what is going to happen. They are looking forward to seeing blood spilled. Cassius circles the man like a lion circling his prey. Then he attacks. He punches the man in the jaw, then slices him in the ribs with a spear. The man cries out and falls to the ground. Cassius stands over him and looks to the crowd for a signal. The crowd roars with their thumbs pointed down. Cassius hefts his spear with a triumphant sneer and holds it over his opponent. I hear a sickening squelch as Cassius brings the spear down. I look with horrified curiosity as the man twitches once, twice, then stills. Dead. The crowd cheers, and the applause is thunderous. Cassius pumps his fists in the air. More events follow, and the man's death is soon forgotten in the midst of fights with bears and lions. Cassius saunters over to me, the pleasure on his face obvious. He will be rewarded with a sack of gold coins for today.

"Good show today, eh, Felix?" he asks.

"It was entertaining," I mumble. It is not wise to upset Cassius, not when he can easily fit his meaty hands around my neck.

"I heard the emperor is bringing in a Gaulish barbarian for next week as the main event. He's supposed to announce who is fighting the barbarian tomorrow."

I gulp. The Gauls are known for their brute strength and blood lust. The poor lad chosen to fight him is going to end up lying on the floor of the Colosseum.

The next day, we gather around as our trainer pulls out a scroll. "I have news from the emperor of Rome. Next week he will be sending a Gaulish prisoner to fight in the Colosseum. He asks that the opponent be well matched, since he will be attending the games himself."

The crowd around me murmurs in excitement. It is not every day we get to see a barbarian from the borderlands. And few of us have ever actually seen the emperor. The trainer raises his hand to silence everyone. "After careful deliberation, I have chosen a fighter. Felix Pontex Gaius, you have been chosen to fight the Gaulish warrior in front of the emperor and the crowds of Rome."

Fear bubbles in the pit of my stomach. After the crowd disperses, I hurry toward the trainer. "Why me?" I ask frantically. "Why not Cassius? He is our best fighter. I am nothing compared to him."

"The emperor will be attending the event, and we need to put on a good show. Cassius would be too predictable; he would crush the Gaul. You on the other hand"—he looks at me with a maniacal glint in his eye—"are at the Gaul's level. A fight between you two shall be quite entertaining for the emperor."

With that, the trainer stalks off leaving me to contemplate my fate alone. I have no doubt that what is being asked of me is impossible. I have never even fought another human in the games before. Usually it is mad boars and the occasional lion. Even killing those was almost unbearable. I spent the hours afterward upending the contents of my stomach into a bucket. I shiver at the thought of having blood on my hands. A battle like this will be a fight to the death. Only one of us will walk out of the arena alive, and I'm not sure I have the strength or the willpower to make sure it's me.

Fight day has arrived. I have trained all week, but nothing could prepare me for the sight of my opponent. He has red and blue stripes running down his face and huge muscles. At least I am tall enough to look him in the eye.

Trumpets blow. The emperor has arrived, and he stands in his box, the golden wreath on his head glimmering in the sunlight. He raises his glass, and the fight begins. My opponent swings at me with his spear. I duck, and my body kicks into survival mode. We both trade blows for what seems like hours until he finally slashes me in the arm with his spear. I grunt. The wound burns like fire. My mind is racing. My opponent is stronger, but I am lighter and faster. I dart around him and swipe my spear across the back of his knees. He falls to the ground. The crowd, sensing bloodshed, starts to cheer. I pin him to the ground, my spear pointed at his chest. The crowd points their thumbs down, signaling me to go in for the kill. I am about to push the spear down, when I look into my opponent's eyes. I see fear, but also acceptance. He knows his end is near. He doesn't want to be here any more than I do. I grip my spear tightly and close my eyes, but all I can think about is the blood on my hands and the look in his eyes. I throw my spear to the ground.

The audience is silent for a moment, unable to comprehend what just happened. Soon enough though, I am faced with an onslaught of boos echoing from the walls of the

Colosseum. I stand there unsure of what to do. As far as I know, no gladiator has refused to kill his opponent before. Suddenly the emperor stands up and the crowd falls silent. The emperor whispers something to a guard next to him. The next thing I know I am being hauled by the guards up to the emperor's box.

"Hey," I say, trying to wriggle out of the guards' grip. "Let me go!"

In response the guards throw me to the floor at the feet of the emperor.

"What is your name, boy?" the emperor asks me.

"Felix Pontex Gaius, your majesty." I keep my head down as I speak, not daring to meet the emperor's eyes.

"Well, Felix Pontex Gaius, after today's events, it seems to me that you do not enjoy being a gladiator."

"No, no, sir." My voice trembles as I speak. "I don't enjoy killing."

"Is that so?" the emperor looks at me with intrigue. "Well then how did you come to be a gladiator? I can't imagine you volunteered."

"My family couldn't pay the taxes, so they sold me to the trainer."

"I see," says the emperor, rubbing his chin. "Well, I think we should get you out of this dreadful situation at once."

I freeze waiting for the punishment to come. How else was I getting out of this situation?

Instead I hear the emperor say, "You seem like a compassionate and honest man, Felix. Jupiter knows I need more of that in my senate. I need people like you who understand the lives of my citizens and are willing to stand up for their rights. And most important of all, I need someone who not only dreams of great things but is willing to fight for them."

I pinch myself; this was something out of a dream.

For as long as I could remember, I had dreamed about the senate. For the first time, I dare to look up. "What are you saying, your majesty?"

The emperor looks at me, and although his eyes are a cold blue, he has a warm smile. "I'm saying that perhaps your place is not here in the arena but in the senate. You shall become one of my aids for now, and we shall see what happens from there. Do you accept my offer?"

"Oh yes, your majesty, I would be honored." I could hardly contain my excitement.

The emperor smiles. "Very good, Felix, have a seat." He gestures to an ornate chair next to his. "After the games, you shall collect your things and come with me, but for now enjoy the view."

I gingerly took a seat in the chair. For the first time I looked down into the arena instead of up at the crowd.

Perhaps there was still hope. I would start off as the emperor's aid, but who knows, maybe I would get a promotion, and someday become a senator. I would be able to help others who had been stuck in my position and forced to fight against their will. The emperor chose me because of my honesty, and I would use it in the senate for the people of Rome. The real fight begins now.

So Many Questions

Arya Kamath

The full moon was high, her sacred light reflecting off the clear and crystal waters that spilled down the marble contours of the town fountain. The fountain was a symbol of such beauty in the small 1880s town, a pillar of joy and radiance. It bonded the farthest corners of the little town in friendship, brotherhood even. For twenty-five-year-old Amelia Anne Sullivan, it was the place where the course of her life changed forever.

Her nights progressed in mindless simplicity. She took comfort in the lack of change. Constancy had always been something that Amelia found comfort in, especially when her Lucas wasn't there to help her through the unsteady. After her supper, she'd go for a stroll around the town fountain, basking in the bright moonlight and enjoying the fall wind as it whipped her blonde hair in a halo around her thin face. She would light her lantern and read a chapter by the firelight, immersing herself in the enrapturing thrills of a good book.

Just as she was about to press on with her book, she heard hoofbeats. After setting her lantern down, she picked up her thick book and held it in front of her in self-defense. She'd be prepared to bring the object down on anyone who might attempt to hurt her.

"Wh-who's there?" she cried out, voice trembling.

"Don't be fearful, ma'am."

She looked to the direction of the voice and sighed in relief, putting her book down. There was a flash of platinum blond, and she knew exactly who it was.

"Officer, you gave me quite a fright! What are you doing here?"

He dismounted his sorrel mare, taking off his hat, a deep

frown on his face.

"Officer, what's happened?" she asked him cautiously, the timbre of her voice low and affrighted. The sullen look on his gaunt face told her all she needed to know, though she was hoping with all her might that it wasn't true.

"We just received a telegram, Mrs. Sullivan. From army headquarters." Nervously, the older man ran his fingers through his platinum-blond hair. It was really a trademark for the well-known man. In that little town, that rare shade of blond could only belong to one person.

"And?" she asked, fearing the worst. She clutched the book to her chest, a part of her hoping that the book would shield her, provide an armor to the devastating blow that she knew was coming, but desperately hoped could be avoided. Perhaps her emotional injury would be just a flesh wound rather than an excruciating stab to her bosom.

"I'm afraid that I have to inform you that...your husband, Sergeant Lucas Sullivan, passed away late this evening. He was so young, lively, it seems such a horrible shame. He died most valiantly, saving the lives of many townspeople as he pushed them out of the way of a falling oak tree in a storm. I offer you my condolences. He was beloved by this town."

It was true. Lucas Giles Sullivan was much beloved by the town, more so than Amelia was. He was the golden boy, the one destined for greatness, the one who would make it out of their small town. Joining the army had only been a means to an end for him, a way to make money so that he could attend medical school. His wealthy aunt Eleanor (who was sweeter on him than her own children) had offered to make the transaction for him, but her righteous Lucas had refused, claiming it would weigh heavy on his conscience. His morals were always unbudgeable, as tight as the steel cords on the ship that he had left on just one month ago.

She should've known that the very thing that made him so

exalted would be the catalyst for his demise. It would have been one thing if he had died in action. It would've hurt less. But the fact that he perished simply because of his choice to be a good person yet again, that was the deepest wound. A selfish part of her whispered that she wished that those accursed townsfolk had died after all if it meant that her husband might've returned back to her arms, safe and sound as he should have been. Another deplorable part of herself conflicted with the selfish part, whispering that he probably hadn't spared a thought to her before risking his life for mere strangers. After all, what was she compared to them?

"What?" she whispered, her voice not being able to muster an ounce of strength. The wind was knocked out of her as if somebody had punched her in the gut. No, that wasn't the right metaphor. It was as if a thousand muscular men had red-hot iron knives that penetrated her stomach every moment of every minute. "No, this can't be." She shook her head in pure and simple denial.

"I'm sorry, Mrs. Sullivan. I'll leave you now." He mounted the horse and rode away.

She had so many questions. Where were they? Did they find his body? Who were these privates and could she meet them?

The news didn't sink in for a long time. She went home and had a cup of tea and indulged in a biscuit or two.

The next day, she walked to the schoolhouse and taught her students as normal, a numb ache persisting. She wondered what was wrong with her. She only felt a dull ache, no sensation to scream or cry like normal. It was finally on the third day—right in the middle of work—when it happened.

"Now, can anyone tell me the average height of an-an, o-oak tree…?" she stammered, the words *oak tree* barreling into her like someone had just pummeled her with one of her own textbooks.

"Seventy feet, Mrs. Sullivan!" Annie Irving piped.

Mrs. Sullivan, Amelia thought, though her entire reason for it was gone. Breath escaped her, and the burning sensation in her eyes signaled that, finally, the impact of three days of denial and grief was flooding back to her.

"C-correct, Annie," she stammered, giving the redhead a strained smile. As she felt moisture start to build in her eyes, she knew that she couldn't hold on for much longer.

"Class is dismissed early for today," she said hurriedly, picking up her teacher's bag and putting the books inside in one swoop. On a second thought, knowing she'd have to make preparations, she continued. "And until further notice. Your homework is to read the next ten pages of your reader to your family. Goodbye."

As the students leisurely collected their papers together, she shoved everything she needed into her tote and all but sprinted out the door, moving faster once she was out the door. She needed to get home.

Where was home for her anymore? Previously, her home was the boy she'd grown up with, fell in love with, married five years ago. Was the house they'd chosen together home without him? Would she ever feel joy in her house knowing that a phantom of him wandered its halls?

She had so many questions.

That didn't matter now. The hollow place was the only place she could go.

Running back with tears spilling out of her eyes, either from the crippling grief or the chilly autumn wind, she finally got to her quaint little house and slammed the mahogany door, discarding her coat on the couch and running to her—*their* bedroom. After she slammed that door also, her eyes landed on a small object that made her temper flare like a bushfire.

Sitting on the ebony desk, there was a small painting in a frame. A young man with deep-set hazel eyes that shone emerald in the light, with a glorious mop of dark curls, smile brighter than a star in a suit. He was closely holding a woman a head shorter than him. She was a willowy woman with rippling strawberry-blonde waves. Her erratic stormy gray eyes were alight with laughter, one hand on his shoulder and the other hanging loose by her side, brushing her lacey white dress.

It was their wedding day. Their blasted wedding day. She picked up the portrait and had an overwhelming urge to throw it against the wall most unbecomingly. She almost did, swinging her arm to shatter it like her heart, but she was interrupted.

Someone had knocked at her door. After setting the portrait down on the desk, Amelia trudged over to open it.

Standing there was a young man with olive-toned skin and hazel green eyes, dark brown curls matted beyond hope. His stature wasn't confident and easy as it had once been. It was tense and rigid. His usually firm muscles had depleted, leaving him gaunt and emaciated, every bone in his body visible. He was in a plain white shirt and brown pants, caked with something dark brown: mud, blood, or both. She gasped shakily. Could it be it was really him or had she started to hallucinate?

"L-Lucas, I thought…"

His eyes were crazed, a mad look in his usually kind eyes. "Run," he whispered hoarsely, his voice cracked like his grime-stained skin.

She had so many questions for her love.

None of them were answered.

As soon as he had finished uttering those words, his eyes snapped open with shock, then pain. He staggered on her doorstep, fresh crimson soaking through his shirt, a tiny piece of alloy lodged square in the middle of his chest. He started to fall, his heart stuttering to a slow stop along with her will to live.

As she darted outside, she could spot nothing, or so it seemed. His killer had fled.

But then...

There was a flash of platinum blonde, and she knew exactly who it was.

The Silent Spectator

Dia Bhojwani

The biting winter air stung my cheeks, turning them ruddy. It was one of those astonishingly clear days, the sun's weak, watery light doing nothing to offset the bleakness of the colorless sky. I loved to walk down this street, far away from the commercialized chaos and cacophony of High Street. It had a quiet, unassuming beauty, the stately oaks and sycamores bowing their verdant heads over the pavement, the antique brass signs of the stores gleaming atop of soft red brick. I looked around me, at the old men with their shriveled, prunelike faces beneath soft felt hats, and at their placid wives with silvery ringlets as they walked to the duck pond at the end of the street, the dazed looking mother pushing her gurgling infant in a bright red stroller, blinking as if she hadn't seen the sun for eons, at the timid, mousy schoolgirl walking back from Arlington's Used Bookstore, a weighty bag of books on her skinny white arm, wire-frame glasses sliding down her nose. They all smiled as they passed each other, smiled wryly as if they shared a secret, which they all did. The secret of serenity, of a peace found not on a yoga mat besides an essential oils diffuser, not in a den of ill repute inhaling fumes and giving yourself up to the arms of strangers, but in a clear winter morning on a quiet street, in tattered books and duck ponds. I inhaled the crisp winter air, and I felt nearly whole, so close to the unrestrained pleasure of being alive.

The smell of melting butter and tender meat tantalized me, pulled me in like a fish on a line. I stopped as I reached the Café Florian. The paint peeled away in strips from the light green windows, revealing the pale wood underneath. A modest establishment, with wide windows, pleasant waiters, and an excellent roast duck with plum sauce that I had once reveled in. Now I peered through the glass, my eyes adjusting to the dim interiors of the café. Not many people were awake this early, but the café had still drawn a sparse crowd, mostly old couples enjoying a heap of steaming waffles and in-house maple syrup after a leisurely stroll, a middle-aged woman with fading blonde hair reading the newspaper over a ham and cheese sandwich, and a couple in a corner, the woman's back turned to me. Hands clasped over the table, entwined like climbing roses. The woman turned, briefly, to the waiter, gave him a flash of her megawatt smile. My fingers clenched painfully as I recognized my wife.

My breath caught in my throat, remained there. I couldn't be mistaken—how could I? My eyes knew the contours of her sylphlike features by heart, my hands knew the slope of her shoulders and the feel of her taut, freckled skin, my ears her laughter, her whispers. Yes, that was her, turning to the waiter and giving him that smile like the sun had come out and was shining just for you, a sheet of mahogany hair falling straight till her slender waist. I felt as though I had been vigorously punched in the stomach. She turned back to the man as the waiter walked away, laughed at something he said. He wasn't what I expected, this man. He was a faded, academic type. She must have met him at the university. Lean and rangy, brown hair tousled by the wind, plaid jacket rumpled, his eyes crinkling at the edges as he looked at her like she hung the moon in the sky. She gestured wildly, nearly knocking her glass of water over. Exuberant, bright-eyed, infinitely enthralling. Not what you would expect of a cold-blooded murderer.

I stepped through the doorway, my heart pounding in my chest like a drum. They didn't look up as I entered, engrossed in their conversation and each other. Her back was to me, and on the table, I could see their intertwined hands. She wasn't wearing her wedding ring, of course. Long, slender, and brown, pianist's hands. I knew well what terrible things those oh-so-lovely hands were capable of. As I neared their table, tucked back in a corner of the room, I was able to hear snippets of their conversation.

"So, what did he do again?" A low voice, impeccable pronunciation. He was well brought up, likely from a prep school. Very unlike my drawled syllables, my Tennessee twang.

"Why do you want to know?" A voice I can only liken to the ringing of church bells, calling men to worship at her altar, like golden sunlight and rich warm honey. I turned and saw her face in full view. Despite our ten years together, despite everything she had done, she still took my breath away, sent adrenaline pumping through my veins, making me feel capable of running a marathon, climbing a mountain, swimming the length of the English Channel. Skin like warm, creamy coffee, rich and brown, wide doe eyes with long, dusty lashes, a sloping, aquiline nose. Her proud, upright bearing, her energy and endless vigor set her apart from any other women in a room, a rose among thorns. So full of life, yet so capable of taking it away.

"I'm just interested. He was a writer, wasn't he?"

"Not a good one."

Her words lacerated me, tore my flesh away in strips. She said that she had loved my stories, didn't care that they didn't sell, that we lived off her money from the university.

"You're always asking about him! Honestly, sometimes I think you're more in love with him than you are with me." A pout of her rosebud lips.

He smiled at her, his entire being suffused with love. It nearly killed me to see the sheer force of it. "Impossible."

She leaned forward, kissed him gently. I longed for the earth's fissures to crack open, for me to fall through, down, down, down, falling into the abyss for eternity, anything but watch this.

The waiter came, plates of steaming hot food balanced on trays, and as she turned to greet him, she saw me over his shoulder. Her eyes widened at the sight of me, consumed with pain, my hands slack at my shoulders, my knees weak. Then they narrowed, those doe eyes that had enchanted me so, that had looked straight into mine as she drove a paring knife though my chest, that watched me, emotionless, as I choked on my own blood on our kitchen floor, waiting for my gurgling to end, to take me to the river, weigh my pockets down with rocks and watch my corpse sink. It was only then, in my final moments, that I saw that there was never anything behind those eyes, that when the mask dropped, there was nothing but a leaden face, a waxen mannequin. She had hated me with a burning fury, hated me for my inability to give her a child, to provide, to be successful, my weakness for drink. She hated me still. So, we stood there, suspended in the silken ropes of time, woman and ghost, looking at each other, a story that took ten years to tell. Few people can look a ghost in the eye and say, with their gaze, "I regret nothing." She turned away from me, to the man that she loved, as I stood, voiceless, a walking shadow, a bloated corpse at the bottom of a river.

Is it odd that I loved her still?

Discovering Reality

Natalia Gala

August 25, 2699 was an important day for science. It was the day the we, the scientists at Total Control Enterprises, broke the boundaries of time and succeeded in bringing three "faces of the past" forward to our present.

We had worked tirelessly for months, coordinating together with multiple AI programs in an attempt to reach our goal before the century was done. This was a discovery worthy of the history books—a discovery found eye to eye with that of light speed travel, teleportation, or immortality. The prior two had long since been achieved—the latter was to be our next groundbreaking project.

I remember walking into the hall where they first brought our three test subjects. As the head scientist, it was my job to extend our company's greetings and explain to them the cause of their sudden misplacement. Their eyes seemed to shine with unease, their voices shook in fear, they glanced around like tiny, scared pigeons… I focused my attention on subject number three, who was a young woman by the name of Alexandra Peterson. Born in the year 1883, she was the eldest of our recruits.

The next three months were a blur. I spent countless hours teaching Alexandra how to get around in our great, modern society, and she in turn spoke to our resident historians and gave them a firsthand account of her life as a farmer in the prairies. Her former life, it turned out, had been immensely difficult—whether she had to survive the chills of winter, fight off hungry wolves, or survive a bout of sickness, there was always one hardship or another.

I saw how she lit up when I showed her our replicating technologies (they prevented starvation), our teleportation stations (they allowed you to go anywhere you wanted to), the medical scanning beams that we set up around every street corner (to prevent outbreaks of disease), and our neural programmers (which allowed you to program yourself with immense quantities of knowledge without having to manually "learn" anything at all).

She commented, on numerous occasions, that our world was "perfect." I had no choice but to agree with her.

It is now April 5, 2700. I have not spoken to Alexandra in over four months. We let her loose and told her to travel around the planet. For the first time ever, we have gained the opportunity to ask someone from the past what they think of the way we have governed Earth. My curiosity overwhelms me. I sit in the hall where I first met Alexandra and wait, once again, for her arrival. I trust she will have nothing but positive feedback.

Once the day is over, perhaps I will take her to accompany me to the city gardens. They sport a vast variety of holographic trees and plants, all of which are now extinct—I am sure that she will feel right at home in such a historic place. I go there every day after work, and it is simply beautiful. Reality could not have been more perfect.

Later

Alexandra sits in the chair opposite to mine and fidgets with her long, auburn hair. She still wears it in the traditional woven fashion, but has seemed to otherwise acclimatize to the modern way of life.

I smile at her. She does not smile back.

"Is everything all right?" I ask, leaning back in my seat and making myself comfortable.

She studies me for a moment with her big brown eyes and

then, all of a sudden, *laughs.*

"I was really happy at first. Everything seemed flawless, faultless, *easy*… I couldn't see anything wrong with it. But the longer I stayed here, Lucy, the more I realized—and am *still* realizing—just how much I miss home."

"You miss having to get up at six a.m. to feed the pigs and later kill the very pigs you cared for?" I raise an eyebrow. "Life in your era was brutal! You had to read to *learn* information, you had to *travel* for *hours* or even *days* or *weeks*… How can you *possibly* miss something like that?"

"It was hard," she replies. "I *know* it was hard. But maybe the fact that it was hard was what made it so fulfilling. You had to *work* to meet your goal, and once you met that goal, you felt like you'd won over the world. But it's not just that. Back then, people *cared* about other people. Now, everything's so… distant. I rarely talk to anyone face-to-face. It's like I'm alone, but at the same time it's so *crowded* and…" She shakes her head. "It was just more *human* and *natural* back then."

"You mean dirty," I counter. "It was *dirty* and *chaotic*. You didn't know when it was going to start raining. Weather was unpredictable—*everything* was unpredictable!"

"Yeah," Alexandra agrees, "but sometimes unpredictable is a good thing. I hate how predictable things are now. There are no surprises—not even good ones. Back in my day, you went out for a picnic and maybe it rained. But that was *fun*! It was *fun* to get surprised, to run back home as fast as you could, laughing with your friends and families…"

"But what *about* your friends and families?" I ask, getting more puzzled by the second. "If one left to go to the city or on vacation, you couldn't call them. You didn't know where they were or what they were doing. Didn't you miss them?"

"I *did*," Alexandra states, "and that was what made my time with them so precious. Everyone today takes everything for granted. I'll say it again—back in my time, people and places were just more…natural. You lived in the moment, because you had no other choice. 'Tomorrow' wasn't necessarily a given. That made you value life—*enjoy* it and *live* it. And don't even let me get started on the trees and plants—you have destroyed *everything*!"

"The holographic gardens and forests we have today are a lot better," I point out. "They can't catch fire, you can program them the way you want to… No weeds or dead trees, either. Those are all gone. Our methods are flawless."

"Exactly!" Alexandra exclaims. "Nothing should be *perfect*! Look up the stars—the one thing you *haven't* destroyed is what's out *there*, in space! Are the stars organized in an orderly and 'perfect' fashion? NO! And that's exactly what makes them so beautiful, Lucy. They're wild and free. Have you ever walked home after work without your head in your *phone*? Have you ever *walked* instead of *teleported* to where you needed to be?"

"No," I murmur, suddenly understanding. "There's no point…*is* there?"

"Today, when you go home, look around. Do that for me, all right? *Look* at your city. *See* it for the first time. Teleporting is a shortcut—you, and not just you, but *everyone* is living life through a magnifying glass. Total Control Enterprises is exactly what its name suggests, and that's not a good thing."

I nod slowly and sigh. "All right."

That Afternoon

The streets are unbelievably crowded. Everyone around me is staring at their phones, relying on only their resident AIs to prevent them from crashing into anyone else. I've never noticed this before, but it turns out that nobody is talking—everyone is just looking down, tap-tapping away into oblivion. I haven't noticed it before because I was exactly the same way. But now, seeing it for myself, well…

It's scary. I don't know exactly why, but it *is*.

The only reason anyone is walking at all is because they have to switch between two different teleportation stations. It's not long before I exit the crowds and find myself wandering, all alone among buildings that seem to touch the sky. Since nobody ever walks here, the skyscrapers are no longer "nice." They are just tall, square things, 3-D printed, and each identical to the next. I realize, all of a sudden, that I have no idea which one is *mine*!

I always teleported up to my apartment, and I used a holographic scene to replace the view from my windows. And now that I am not using my AI guide, I also see one other thing—I am completely *lost*.

Am I really so dependent on technology? Do I really rely on it for every single little thing? I'm a scientist, but how much of what I know do I really know? I just programmed my doctorate right into my head, and that was *it*. It wasn't really "me" who unlocked time travel, then—*was it?*

I'm not enjoying this technology-free existence. It gives me too much time to…*think*.

All of a sudden, a flash of color among the stark white landscape of the city makes me stop in my tracks. I rush over to the side of the sidewalk and drop down to my knees.

There, amid the loose decorative pebbles, is something unexpected—something *unpredicted*.

It's a flower—a real, live flower.

I've never seen a real flower before. But the feeling of wonder that I get when I brush my fingers across its cool, damp petals, so beautifully imperfectly violet and blue, so much more wild and breathtaking than any hologram…

It's *real*. Could it be that is the first time I have ever touched the real world?

Poles Apart: Kiska

Kendall Conway

Only those with inherited riches and insensitive, lacquered hearts may rest behind the polished walls. Only the sanguinary receive a home enveloped by blue diamonds, guarded by loyal cretins.

I am permitted to stare at the peace from a distance before returning to my hovel made of supplies gathered from the earth. And while Swayers inside the polished walls thrive in their trades of jadeite, I use what lies below my feet, and I eat what soars above the platinum strands on my head.

"An aberration!" they shouted. "Get rid of the malformation before we're plagued!"

But now, even thirty miles away from the perimeter, I can hear the boom of the announcement speakers. They tell the tale of the paperwhite-haired child who grew up in secret.

Because she was different, her and her family were executed. The autarch's, Ephraim's, version of the story is entirely true—apart from the fact that I am not dead.

I suppose schoolchildren are told this story in efforts to remind them all to remain exactly the same. After all, Inferiors are easier to control that way. And considering all Swayers—Inferiors and Ephraim himself—practice fire generation and weaponry, it is vital to an autarch's protection of their reign to restrain diversity. So what a *shame* it would be if the aberration rose from the dead to avenge her family.

Ephraim has sent military Swayers into the forests outside the kingdom for the last fifteen years. I am starved from revenge, and I am well trained with the help of wild creatures made of furs and gnashing teeth. Every two days, Ephraim's five Swayer assassins march with stealth into the dry wood and brown grass. Their palms face toward the sun, charging their skins to ready their flames. Today, I stay perched in the thickest tree I could find near their path to search for me.

Before my family was slaughtered, they all tried to teach me how to use my flames in private. We never progressed. But despite my strange inability, I've found other ways to conquer Swayers. I have strength unlike any other, more self-reliance than Ephraim's dependent soldiers, and an anger more flammable than any fire.

My mother's screams of terror. My father reaching out to his fifteen-year-old sons and his wife for one last embrace. My brothers staring at me, both warm and kind and silent so they could sacrifice themselves for me. And I hid. I hid in the street well, where they all told me to stay. I could only peek up far enough to watch their lives be publicly stolen before running away underground, tears blinding me. I was only a girl then, but it doesn't excuse my cowardice. Now, I am no longer idle. Even without fire, I can feel it burning inside. I feel the flames licking up my stomach and into my throat, tasting vile. My fingertips dig into the tree branch until they split and bleed. Their footsteps are echoing now. They're so close. I can smell their palms smoking.

There was so much pain in my heart for so many years. I cried so many tears. My throat became raw from screaming in agony on the days Swayers weren't searching. No more. My parents' and my brothers' lives were not taken in vain. They mean something, and their deaths meant something.

Before I can jump on one of the Swayers, my branch cracks beneath me. I don't falter when the lead Swayer launches a burning ball of red and orange in my direction. Their eyes are full of shock and fear and excitement all at once.

"We were really beginning to think you were a myth," one jokes.

A malicious smirk dances on my lips. "You are *really* going to wish I were."

Immediately, I leap from my branch to a tree across the path. My skin warns me that their flames are close with the alarming sensation of heat. One hit could brand me with the mark of murderers. But again, I am not afraid. My thirst to slit their throats only enhances as they continue to attack me as best as they can. I waltz and twirl with equipped grace in the trees. Their frustration increases as well, and in turn, they dial in more precisely.

One of the women eyes me just at the right time, nailing my ribs with a dagger made of the forest's enemy. I fall from my height in the trees, landing on my back with a thud that steals the breath from my body. All that fuels me is the image of my family's death. I limp up, looking behind me to see them cheering and running to claim their hunted prize. But I hide behind a fallen log, hand pressed onto my charred and bloody gash. I steady my breathing and try not to grunt as one gets too close, lunging onto him and cracking his neck quickly. His eyes stare at nothing, and his hands sizzle out as the fire dies inside.

"Oren!" the woman who struck me cries. Her eyes lock onto mine with fury. "You filthy aberration!"

I force myself to forget about the pain in my side as I stand up and sprint away from the four Swayers left in my wake. After half a mile, I dive into tall grass, evading their sight once more. As they near, another man's voice can be heard dialing for more Swayers. More soldiers bearing flames to scorch my body. That's exactly what I need.

One woman and the guy radioing for backup get closer. I grab one foot of each, yanking them to the ground. One of them, out of fear, lights a fire in the dry grass. I roll on top of the woman, grabbing my homemade knife out of my pocket and jabbing her in the neck. She holds on to the hole with both hands to save herself, but to no avail. The man comes after me next, but I throw an elbow into his nose before spinning him around as a shield for another soldier to melt his face away.

Two more are left dead as I run again.

I can see the opening of the trees, where light sheds through to signal an entrance to Inferior Lake. This is the only place where Inferiors are allowed outside of the walls with guards supervising them. Here is where I plan to expose myself to daily Inferiors doing their washing and cleaning and water collecting. Here they will see I am *not* dead.

The last male Swayer grabs me backward by the wrist and throws me into the sand just outside of the clearing. I groan and grasp my side, squeezing my eyes shut as I throw my boot into his knee. He collapses, fire missing me as he cries out. I scramble to stand before yielding my knife in the air and lunging it into his skull with a scream. Several Inferiors and guards stare and scream in terror.

I haven't been around so many people in nearly two decades.

"I am Kiska, the aberration! I am alive!" I shout, voice shaking. My skin is covered in blood, and I can feel the air become chilled instantly. It must be cold by the lake. "They can't kill me!"

They all gasp, murmuring fearful words.

Before I can keep stability, the last Swayer standing tackles me from behind. She flips me over, pinning my arms to the sand. I struggle against her but then laugh, blood spilling from my lips. I stain my skin crimson. Everything is cold.

"They saw me. It's on the kingdom's broadcast. I win, evil witch," I spew.

She roars before lifting her hand and pressing into me with a blaze so hot it should melt right through me. Only it doesn't. I don't feel heat. In fact, I feel the exact opposite. And it feels so good. So right. I look down to see her fist locked in a block of ice.

Ice.

"What are you, you *freak*?" she screams, frantically trying to escape the ice. It isn't melting as she tries to use her free hand of flames.

I can feel it coursing through me. The ice belongs in my veins.

"Get her!" a soldier shouts.

They start to charge toward me. I feel my heart racing, and my breath leaves white clouds, ignoring the heat of the summer. I see Mom. Dad. Tysek. Perron. They were taken away from me. Murdered. I will never let their memory fade.

I scream.

I scream so loud the earth cracks and the trees shake. A cold I have never felt before shocks my spine.

The world falls still.

My eyes open.

No soldier or guard is alive, bodies frozen and purple.

Inferiors stare at me in fear, huddled together in amazement.

And I look out beyond myself.

I froze the lake.

I froze the forest.

I froze the kingdom.

Her Breakaway

Evelyn Kelly

I walk grimly with the cheer squad out of the gymnasium and down the school hallway. We were sure that 1969 would be the year our basketball team went undefeated. That just goes to show how wrong you can be.

"We should have won," our captain, Linda, gripes, her hand on her hip. "We're a *much* better team than those Tigers."

I feel the need to correct her. "We were lazy on defense. And Keith didn't set up any plays."

She turns to me and scowls, and that's when I remember that she and Keith are going steady. "Isn't it your dad's job to decide what the team needs to do?"

"Well, yeah, he's the coach—"

Linda cuts me off. "Then maybe you should focus less on basketball and more on our pyramid."

I feel my face get hot as I look down at the swollen bruise on my elbow. I have never fallen off a single pyramid in practice, but of course it happens in my very first game.

"I hope that won't happen again," Linda continues with a condescending smile. She places her hand over her heart, mocking sympathy. "You must be *humiliated*."

I'm not sure how to respond. I think back to our junior high days. Since we lived on the same street, Linda and I were inseparable. She'd come over to my house to steal a few hours of calm away from her rowdy brothers, and we'd bike to the Burger Shack for milk shakes.

That changed when she became a cheerleader, though, in our freshman year. Suddenly, she was popular, and I wasn't. She glowed at the center of a circle of admirers, and I was left out. My doorbell never rang, and my bike sat neglected in my garage.

In a pathetic attempt at popularity, I tried out for cheerleading, too. Every year. I was rejected three times, but I finally made it this year.

Apparently, though, Linda and I will never be friends again.

Awoken from my daydream, I realize I've stopped walking to think, and the rest of the squad is ten yards ahead of me.

Alone, I study the hallway bulletin board of school flyers. One catches my eye. *GIRLS INTRAMURAL BASKETBALL LEAGUE*, it screams in bold letters on the top.

I blink, making sure I've read that correctly. But yes, it does read *girls*. Odd. I've never heard of high school sports for girls. The coach is my history teacher, Miss Robinson. I wonder what she knows about basketball.

"Are you thinking about joining, Debbie?" As if I've summoned her, Miss Robinson appears behind me. She's wearing a crisp white blouse, a brown pencil skirt, pearl earrings, and her bobbed hair perfectly flipped out. I struggle to picture her with a clipboard, barking at her players to *hustle* and *get back on defense* like my dad.

"Basketball seems pretty rough, and maybe a little...wrong for girls," I reply, glancing from her to the flyer and back again.

"Well, you know, being feminine and playing sports aren't mutually exclusive," says Miss Robinson. "Contrary to what some people think. The reason most girls don't play sports is because they don't have the opportunity."

Her comment suddenly gives color to a topic I've always seen as black and white. Why haven't I ever gotten to play sports? Simply because I was born a girl? I pause. "Well, I'm a cheerleader, anyway."

Miss Robinson rubs my arm delicately, giving me a

sympathetic smile. "I know."

"I'll think about it," I tell her, and truthfully, I will. I'd never given much thought to the unjust and absurd reality that if I were a boy, I'd most likely be our starting center, playing for my dad. Instead I'm stuck on the sidelines waving pom-poms, desperate to cheer my way into Linda's fan club.

She gives me a wide grin. "Super! See you on the court."

***

"Basketball?" Dad questions me as we head home in our Lincoln Continental. "You want to play basketball?"

I nod. "Miss Robinson's forming an intramural league."

"I think I heard something about that." Dad turns his eyes back to the road and whistles. "Margaret Robinson has some...interesting ideas."

"Interesting?"

"Well," Dad says casually, "you've never played basketball before. Probably none of your other friends have, either. The fact that Miss Robinson thinks a bunch of girls will play now is pretty interesting."

"Well, I want to play," I reply, crossing my arms. "And maybe I would have before if there had been a basketball team. We used to play all the time in the driveway."

"Debbie…" he says, chuckling softly. "You know that playing with me wasn't *actual* basketball, right? Playing the entire game is a lot of running up and down the court—it's very tiring. You have to be tough." Dad talks to me as if I hadn't sat beside him through eight seasons of coaching.

"Dad. I fell from a pyramid today!" I hold my elbow up to his face, showing him my bruise for emphasis. "Do you want to say I'm not tough again?"

"I didn't say you weren't tough." He sighs. "My answer is no, Debbie. And that's final."

***

The next morning is a Saturday, but I wake up just after dawn. I don't bother changing out of my nightgown. I slip on my Keds and creep into the garage as quietly as I can, in order not to wake Dad.

Our garage is a mess. Since I haven't played basketball for nearly six years, the basketball is probably buried underneath mounds of junk. I wade through boxes of old clothes, my rusted bicycle, broken hula hoops, and jump ropes. Finally, I find my basketball. Flat and misshapen, but I can make do. Giddy with excitement, I skip out to the driveway and begin shooting.

I'm surprised how much more exhilarating it is to shoot a dusty, ancient ball in my sloped driveway than to watch the team play an actual game in our state-of-the-art gymnasium. I shoot again, imagining it as a bird flying from my hands to the hoop. It goes in.

"Debbie?"

Ugh.

I take one more shot, then turn to face Dad. He's already dressed in his usual attire, a gray suit with a tie and matching trousers, his expression cold.

"I need to talk with you," he says sternly.

With no choice but to obey, I slink up to the porch.

"Sit," he commands.

I plunk down on one of our brown chairs and prepare for the lecture.

"I'm not saying, Debbie, that I approve of you quitting cheer just because you fell in your first game. But if you don't like cheer, why don't you try the dance team?"

"I *do* like cheerleading. I just want to try playing basketball for once."

"But if you play basketball—" He pauses and puts his

head in his hands, obviously frustrated. Then he looks up and says, "Debbie, do you want everyone to mistake you for a boy when you have biceps like Keith Parker?"

"Having muscles doesn't make me a boy! Playing sports and being feminine aren't—" I pause as I hastily search my memory for the phrase Miss Robinson said. "Mutually exclusive."

He looks confused. "Mutually exclusive? Where'd you hear that?"

"Miss Robinson told me that."

He shakes his head. "Of course she did." Then he crosses his arms and doesn't say another word.

After a few more moments of silence, I can't take it anymore. "Dad, please. I really want to see what it's like to play basketball."

"I just want you to be safe."

Safe? What does he think I'm doing, registering for the draft? "I'm just playing basketball. If you don't think basketball's safe, then why do you coach?"

"I coach boys. Not girls. Two completely different things."

"Well, they shouldn't be! That doesn't make any sense. You let me play in the driveway. You know I have more knowledge than most of your players. But yet, I can't play."

He looks torn. In silence, I watch his expression morph from anger to surrender and back again. Finally, he exhales loudly. "I'll give you two weeks."

My heart flutters. "Yes!" I jump up and can't help but fling my arms around his neck. "Thank you!"

"You're welcome," he grunts, patting my back lightly. He begins to make his way inside. Without turning, he adds, "But if you start burning your bras, it's over."

I laugh, feeling a little uneasy about my dad saying the

word *bras*.

Basketball isn't something Linda would do, but honestly, I don't care. I'm going to have fun in high school for once. Maybe there will never be a girls' team as celebrated as the boys' team, but if my dad agreed to let me play, then anything could happen. Two weeks isn't long, but it's a small step in the right direction.

I leap from my chair and run to the hoop to shoot again.

Swish.

Tower of Light

Kelsey Pizante

Five years. It has been five years since my sister's death. Five years since I jumped into the choppy aquamarine waters led by a sharp fear in my heart. Five years since my baby sister drowned after I failed to save her. Five years since I began to fear and resent part of my home.

Five years.

The gentle sea breeze tosses my curls into a brown cloud as I stare into the coral sky, the sun slowly stretching its golden glow up from the ocean it hides behind.

The ocean. For five years I have thought of it with disdain. Its predictable yet ever changing pattern of waves tumbling onto the shores of the cliff-maimed Oregon coast. The way it stretches out endlessly as if it owns the whole world.

But in a way, I guess it does.

The ocean certainly controls my life. I look to my right and see my father, always up at dawn, heading down from our small stone house to the lighthouse. He carries the oil from the shed to the top of the lighthouse every morning.

I've lived at Stoneside Lighthouse my whole life. Ever since I could comprehend, I've looked up at our white-bricked, glass-headed lighthouse and wondered why my father was so passionate about keeping it running. Once, when I was about five, I asked him.

"I don't know, Morgana. It's always been what I was made to do. Just like the lighthouse was made to be lit, I was made to light it," was his answer.

I've always looked up to my father because I know what he does, though indirectly, saves lives.

I wish I could say the same.

I head back to our living quarters. I walk in, and my mother is preparing food for the day, and I know I am to help her.

"Even though it's a sad day, Morgana, that does not mean we are going to work less," she says when she notices me. "Now take that dough and knead it."

With a sigh, I pick the mass up and begin to massage it. The pounding of my hands mimics my throbbing heart.

***

Evening falls before I manage to escape my mother and get outside. There is always something else to do. Food always needs preparing. The house always needs cleaning. Clothes always need mending. The only positive thing about the work is that it distracts me from my grief.

I was absorbed in a book, since I, at nine, had just discovered the wonder of reading, but I could still hear Mother and my four-year-old sister playing in the waves. Mother set Marinne down and told us she was going inside to get her sewing.

"Do not go into the water!" she told us sternly.

I didn't notice as Marinne did exactly that, wading deeper. Her sudden scream grabbed my attention though, and I jumped in after her. The waves were rough, and I couldn't get her back to shore before she was pulled under by an undertow.

She never came up.

I haven't touched the ocean since.

"Hey, Ana!"

"Hey, Crew," I answer. I playfully scowl, pretending to hate the nickname I secretly love.

His green-blue kaleidoscope eyes are glinting in the sun. Crew Dylan is an orphan who lives nearby with my uncle, who was a friend of his parents. We've always been friends, bound by the gravitational heartache of tragedy.

Crew looks at me closer, trying to read my expression. He

doesn't have to. He knows me too well. "How are you doing?"

"I'm fine. Well, as fine as I can be."

He nods. "Let's go down to the beach. Watch the sunset. Maybe it will get your mind off everything."

We walk down the well-worn path until we reach the sand, sitting well out of the reach of the waves.

Crew knows about my fear of water. He's known ever since it developed five years ago. What he doesn't know is how badly I want to face it and conquer it. How much I want a victory over the force that took my sister, and, in turn, my courage.

But since it has stolen my courage, the very thing that allows us to face our fears, there's no chance of that.

I sigh and listen to the rolling waves. A distant, otherworldly sound, like a discordant scream, interrupts the steady crashing of the water. But I must be mistaken. I do not believe in things as foolish as ghosts.

"It doesn't seem right," Crew says quietly. "That we get to sit here and watch the sunset for the four thousandth time, when she only got to see it one thousand times."

I look at the sunset. The scarlets, golds, fuchsias, and ceruleans blend together to form a magnificent background for the sinking sun. Too beautiful to represent the end of light.

"Yes. It's not right." My voice is hoarse and faint. "Not right at all." I look over at Crew and find a reason to smile. "Did you do that math in your head?"

"You underestimate my abilities," he says, turning his face to the wind. "I'm something of a math prodigy."

I laugh and look back at the ocean, noting its rather restless behavior. I see something reaching out from the waves.

Is that an arm?

I squint. Sure enough, I see a head struggling to stay above the water. It registers in my mind that there is a person in the water, a person *in danger.*

"Crew!" I shout, pointing.

His eyes widen, and he wastes no time getting in the water. He swims out to the person, flailing and screaming in his life vest. Crew put the person's arm around his own shoulders.

Crew looks at me and yells, "He's bleeding!"

My heart pounds in my ears. "Hurry!"

I have run closer to the ocean than I have dared in years, but I forget to be afraid, thanks to the adrenaline rushing through me.

They try to swim back to shore as choppy swells beat at them. Every stroke Crew makes is thwarted by a wave. Deep down, I know they will never make it.

"Should I get help?" I yell desperately, pacing along the shoreline.

"No time!" Crew gasps for air. "*You* have to help!"

Me? I froze. "I can't! You know I can't!"

"You have to, Morgana!"

They disappear under a wall of turquoise.

I step toward the white foam at the edge of the sand. I push down my fear; there's no time. I wade into the cold water, and everything slows down. My sister's favorite lullaby enters my mind.

There's a tower of light, nestled upon a rocky cliff

Seawater reaches my waist.

Surrounded by

I fall into the waves and pull myself forward with my arms.

Rolling seas and ever changing beauties

My body remembers how to swim as if I'd never stopped.

Fleeing waves of bravery

I reach Crew and the man.

Late maritime ghosts

I grab Crew, my fingers so numb I'm surprised I can grip him.

Floating, gliding, effortlessly sliding

The man's head lolls against his chest as he falls unconscious.

Sailing by a rippling moon

A twist in the tide pushes me back.

Ships in the night, seeking what can only be found

The ocean is not going to have another victory over me.

Seeing, feeling, beholding

The shore is just a few strokes away.

That tower of light

I can stand now, and Crew and I are dragging along the unconscious man.

Tower of light

We're out of the water.

Tower of light.

With the last note of the song, everything returns to a normal pace. The man coughs and opens his eyes as my parents come rushing over. They must have realized we've been gone for too long. Crew holds me, and as they fuss over us, I feel victory through the anguish.

***

Finnley Zale. That's the name of the sailor Crew and I saved. Thanks to my mother's healing, he's now fine, the wound in his side stitched up. He was aboard a steamship when a rogue wave caused it to wreck. We don't know for sure, but we think he's the only survivor.

Survivor.

My sister can never be replaced, but maybe the life I saved can help atone for the one I couldn't. And I can atone for my cowardice by continuing to be brave and keep facing the unbound sea.

Outside, away from all the chaos, I end the day like I started it. Gazing at a horrible, beautiful, powerful force of nature, this time under a canopy of stars. But tonight, I look at it not with fear, but with pride and reverence, the same way I have always looked at our lighthouse, our tower of light.

But the most valuable change is how I look at myself, a force of nature and a tower of light in my own right.

Credo

Olivia A. Duke

OCTOBER 28, 1951
PRAGUE, CZECHOSLOVAKIA

Josef emerges from underground. The flags and propaganda littered throughout his beloved city stir in him a longing for his old, safe home.

Josef remembers that his parents will want to celebrate when he reaches home; it is his birthday. Josef's parents have always told him that his birthday is something significant—October 28, 1918. It was also the day that Czechoslovakia came into existence. His parents always say that date symbolizes strength and perseverance. It was a hopeful day. Then the next war came and with it, persecution. Then the Communists came and with them, persecution. Now all of Eastern Europe is living in a permanent terror; October 28 was far from the end of the pain.

Josef reaches his home and enters to his papa waiting. He looks around and notices *trdelník*—a traditional Czechoslovakian spit cake—sitting in the middle of the table. Josef knows that it is for his birthday. He smiles gently at this.

"Josef," his papa says softly. "You cannot go anymore."

Josef does not break his eyes away from his papa's. He remains still, with a silence stuck in his throat; there is simply nothing to say to such a thing.

"Do you understand?" His papa speaks in a harsher tone now.

Josef tries to bring words forward, yet he does not know where to start.

"He's gone. Do you understand, Josef? He's gone." Josef's papa has tears filling his eyes.

Josef's lips move; nothing comes.

"You know the dangers of going," Josef's papa continues. "I simply do not understand why you find reason in going at all. He's gone. Do you understand, Josef?"

Josef has feared this beyond all measure. He's feared this since they told him what happened.

His papa wanders out, wiping the rapid tears. Josef watches his papa approach his mama and gesture to Josef, still standing by the door. As he gestures, he slowly pushes the *trdelník* to the end of the table, farthest from Josef.

Josef walks to his room and sits on the floor, looking up to the crucifix on the wall. He looks at the wounds on the feet and hands of Jesus.

"How do I live through this, My Lord?" Josef's words tumble out of his mouth. "I cannot hurt my parents, but more so, I cannot hurt You."

He reaches over to a picture on a small table and holds it in his hands.

The picture depicts a man dressed in all black, and at closer glance, he is wearing a cassock—a Catholic priest's clothing. The man in the photo has a joyful smile across his face. On the back of the photo in his papa's writing is:

"Father Jan Schovajsa, 1947."

Father Schovajsa was Josef's uncle—his papa's brother. In 1948, when the Communists came, Father Schovajsa refused to stop saying masses or hearing confessions. He said underground masses for three years, until just two weeks ago, when he went missing. Everyone knew what it meant for someone to go missing—they weren't coming back. They all knew he died for his faith, and that is something Josef looks up to with a strong admiration.

Josef understands his papa's pain. He understands why his papa doesn't want him going out to mass anymore—but he doesn't agree. He will not stand silent in persecution. He will not be lukewarm when God was sending a chance for him to show his love. He would not deny his faith to protect his life when Jesus had given His Life to protect humanity's faith.

Josef hears a soft knock coming from behind the curtain, which proves use as a door. To this, he makes a soft acknowledgment, thus allowing entrance for the waiting.

His mama walks in lethargically—not wanting to have this conversation again. She pushes the curtain closed and sits beside Josef on the floor, looking up at the crucifix.

After a short while of silence, she looks at the picture of Father Schovajsa in Josef's hands.

"Your uncle was a good man," she says eventually.

"I know, Mama," Josef responds.

"He was a priest, Josef."

"Yes, he was."

"Yes."

"I'm not sure I understand, Mama."

"The fact that he continued saying mass does not mean you should keep attending; he was a priest."

"That does not take away his bravery."

"No, of course not."

"I look up to him, yes, but he is seldom my reason for attending mass, Mama. My reason is love."

"I know. I know."

"You taught me to love the Eucharist. How can you take that back?"

"Josef," his mama says firmly. "Your papa and I are not commanding you to disregard your love for the Eucharist."

Josef does not have anything to say.

"Come." His mama gets up and pulls his arm gently. "You must speak with your papa."

Josef holds tight to the floor in a moment of hesitation, then glances at the crucifix and rises to his feet.

He feels himself pushing the curtain open again, but does not see it. His movements are purely habitual. Instead, he sees the Eucharist in front of him, knowing that he must not give it up, no matter what his parents say.

His papa looks up at him from where he is sitting. "You will stop going?" he asks gently.

Josef remains silent.

"Josef, what can we do to convince you?" his papa begs him.

Josef looks into his papa's eyes.

"I think I'd have to die first," he says resolutely.

Josef sees his parents exchange a quick glance.

"Do you understand the pain of losing your uncle?" his papa asks, not looking at Josef.

"Perhaps he's alive—"

"Do not say that, Josef. You know well that he is not."

Josef looks at the floor. He thinks of his uncle—Father Schovajsa.

"Do you remember what he used to say?" Josef asks calmly.

"Your uncle?" his mama asks.

"Yes."

"I'm not sure I know of what you speak."

"Our last name, Schovajsa," Josef says with a less timid voice now. "It means…"

"Hide yourself," his papa says firmly.

Josef nods and smiles softly. "Yes."

His mama and papa look at each other in confusion.

"He always used to comment on that last name. He would say that it meant 'hide yourself,' but that was entirely ironic because Catholics should never hide themselves," Josef explains.

He watches his papa look to his hands.

"He would laugh at the name," Josef continues. "He would always tell me that we had to be humble and hide ourselves in humility; he would interpret our last name that way. He hated the idea of hiding the fact that we are Catholic from others."

Josef watches as his mama and papa look at each other, and he smiles with a hope that maybe they will change their minds.

"I do not want to hide myself, Papa, not in the way he fought against so earnestly. I think he would be more pleased if we went to mass, for which he fought with his life." Josef sits beside his papa. "Remember, Papa, the Communists win if we do not go, but God wins if we do."

Josef's parents stay enwrapped in a silence. Josef prays that this means the end of this long fight.

After a while, he gets up and goes to his room, quickly glancing at his uneaten *trdelník*.

NOVEMBER 30, 1951,
PRAGUE, CZECHOSLOVAKIA

Josef peacefully walks his route to the church. Joy fills his heart as he thinks of the Eucharist he will soon receive. He smiles widely as he walks and holds his rosary.

He stops abruptly as he notices the man standing directly in front of him.

"Where are you going?" The man has a gentle voice, but Josef knows they are not on the same side of this never-ending war.

Josef tries to simply continue walking around the man, but the man will not let him.

"What is that?" The man tries to grab the rosary from Josef's hands, but Josef clutches it close to his chest.

Josef remains utterly silent.

The man studies Josef's face. "You are not one of them…are you?"

"One of whom?" Josef meets the man's eyes now.

"One of those religious." The man scoffs. "A Jew or Catholic or Protestant or another."

"I am Catholic," Josef says resolutely.

"You are a stupid one to admit it." The man grabs Josef by the hair and throws him on the ground.

"Are you an officer, sir?" Josef asks, with pain in his voice.

The man does not respond, but instead pulls out his Prava pistol and puts it against Josef's forehead, who still lies on the ground.

Josef starts taking deep breaths. He thinks of his parents. They will know he died after he goes missing. They never supported his attending mass, but stopped arguing about it last month. He prays that his death will bring them to mass, not further away.

He thinks back to a specific day—his birthday. He never ate his *trdelník*, his favorite dessert. His parents must've gone to great lengths to get it, he thinks. Perhaps his *trdelník* wasn't meant for that day anyway, but today—which he knows will be his real birthday.

He thinks of the Eucharist. He longs for it, but he will not receive it today. Instead he will meet his Creator.

Josef looks into the man's eyes in front of him. They are rough; they do not know their purpose. They do not understand that they are God's creation.

The man fiddles with the trigger and laughs.

"May my life be offered for your conversion and the conversion of our home," Josef says softly. "Credo."

Josef does not look away from the man's eyes, watching the small hesitation in his movements.

With their eyes still locked, the man pulls the trigger.

Tidal Waves

Travis Xue

In the country of Greece, there lived a celebrity swimmer called Tidalus. He was known worldwide for his impressive skill in swimming the most dangerous waters of the world. He lived in Oceana, a city at the edge of the dazzling, yellow seaside of Greece. Studded with gleaming white houses and pastures of lush grass, Oceana was the perfect home for celebrities like Tidalus.

On Mount Olympus, Poseidon admired Tidalus and watched him whenever he could. However, Tidalus became boastful about his skill whenever he beat another star swimmer, and Poseidon was concerned about that.

"He is so professional and I am fond of watching him swim, but he cannot just go around bragging like that," sighed Poseidon.

Two days later, Tidalus was scheduled to compete against Brocherous, the best swimmer in the Greek province Macedonia. Even before the race began, Tidalus pumped his fists into the air, confident that he was going to win, but what happened next shocked everybody. Brocherous defeated Tidalus! Even more surprising, Brocherous had reached the end nearly five minutes before Tidalus had.

That night, Brocherous was having the time of his life, partying the night away. On the other hand, Tidalus sulked back home, unwilling to believe that he had been defeated. However, what nobody knew was that Poseidon had purposely made Tidalus lose by making the water Tidalus was swimming in more choppy and rough than it normally was, giving Brocherous a massive advantage.

"Finally Tidalus has learned his lesson," Poseidon snickered.

Although it seemed like Tidalus had changed, the fact that

he lost only incited stronger feelings of self-pride. He blamed his loss on the water, the weather, and everything but himself.

When it was time for a rematch between the two men, Tidalus was quiet, which the audience found very unusual. The race started normally, but the ending was shocking. Tidalus had beat Brocherous by nearly ten minutes! The audience went berserk when the results were announced while Poseidon remained calm and hopeful. He cared about Tidalus's attitude, not the results of the race.

Tidalus, seeing how enthusiastic the audience was for him, started beating his chest and let gifts from his supporters rain down on him. It was quite obvious that he had not changed.

"I have given Tidalus a chance, and I have tried teaching him a lesson, but now I will have to give him a warning!" shouted Poseidon furiously, banging his trident on the ground.

Poseidon morphed into an elderly woman, entered the mortal world, and walked over to Tidalus's house. Poseidon then knocked on his door.

When Tidalus saw Poseidon, he asked arrogantly, "Who are you to knock on my door?

Disgusted by the rude introduction, Poseidon explained why he came. "I am a seer, Tidalus. I have come not to congratulate you, but to warn you that I have been receiving messages from Poseidon saying that he will curse you if you do not stop being such a braggart."

Tidalus laughed wickedly in response. "How can Poseidon kill me? After all, I am the best swimmer in the history of the world! A showdown like that will make history!"

Seeing that Tidalus refused to follow his advice, Poseidon sternly replied, "I have warned you, and I have tried teaching you, young man, that the past determines the future. Anything that will happen to you later, remember, will have been the result of your decision."

Tidalus continued to laugh and shut the door with a loud *BANG*! Meanwhile, Poseidon, knowing that Tidalus was unwilling to change, could only fly back to Mount Olympus and plot his revenge.

Zeus saw Poseidon the moment Poseidon entered the heavenly gates of Mount Olympus. Zeus saw the pain and fury in Poseidon's face and asked him, "Brother, what is it that is concerning you so much? I have noticed that you have been keeping to yourself lately. Perhaps you need some ambrosia to feel better?"

Poseidon sat down and then began to pour out his tale of woe and exasperation. "Oh, dear brother, the famous, handsome Tidalus has been acting so exultant! I just tried to tell him to stop acting the way he is, but do you know what he did? He started mocking me! We have created humans to be diligent, humble creatures, but look at them now! So pretentious! So selfish!"

By then, Poseidon had started to monologue, and Zeus had to stop him.

"Poseidon, we have been through this before. You have already cursed plenty of people. How different can it be? What makes you think you could not punish Tidalus right now?"

Poseidon protested, "But, Zeus, he is the best swimmer I have ever seen! He is the one human I care about. I adore watching him swim, and I do not dare punish him. My problem, brother, is that I have been thinking about whether I should leave him as he is or punish him. I cannot make up my mind, so please! Please give me some advice on what I should do!"

Zeus, after thinking for a while, replied, "You are right when you said that we have created man to not be this way. Therefore, you must punish him. Putting a curse on Tidalus, or even killing him, will teach the whole race of man a lesson. It is our duty to make sure people live by the proper decorum and that no one falls out of line. So go! Do what is right!"

Before Poseidon left Mount Olympus, he jokingly remarked, "I may have lost my temper, Zeus, but you certainly have not lost your wisdom!"

On Earth, Tidalus was being lectured by Metis, his wife.

"You should not have insulted that seer! Insulting seers is the same as insulting the gods themselves! Frightening as the idea is!" shouted Metis.

"I am the king of swimming if you did not know that! Poseidon may be the god of water, but I am the god of swimming! He could not have killed me even if he tried!" retorted Tidalus.

"And that is the exact type of attitude that gets you killed!" countered Metis.

"I thought you were supposed to be my supporter. But now you are telling me I cannot do what is best for me!" yelled Tidalus.

"I am trying to save your life here, Tidalus! Just because you are privileged does not mean you have the right to behave this way! Plus, bragging will not do anything but hurt you!" shouted Metis.

"Bragging helps me feel confident about myself," said Tidalus, yawning. "Anyway, I have a big race tomorrow from Hydra to Patmos. If I don't get some sleep, I'll lose."

And with that, he excused himself, entered his bedroom, and locked the door. Metis, defeated, retreated toward her own room.

On the day of the race, Tidalus did not believe anything would happen. He was too obsessed with the fact that he was going to beat another rival and could finally deem himself world champion.

On Mount Olympus, Poseidon was secretly watching, ready to slaughter Tidalus. The race was going through the Aegean Sea, a perfect place to strike. As Tidalus neared Patmos, there would be plenty of witnesses, and he could easily manipulate the waters of the Aegean.

"Go!"

The referee's voice shattered the air like a hammer, and

both of the swimmers plunged into the water. Within thirty minutes, Tidalus had almost reached Patmos while his opponent was not even close. This was the moment Poseidon had been waiting for. He conjured up a massive wave until it was powerful enough to knock out a Cyclops, let alone a small pile of bones like Tidalus, and launched it toward Tidalus.

When Tidalus caught sight of the wave, he was chilled to the bone and, panicking, tried to swim out of harm's way. However, it was no use and the wave smashed into him. His body sunk into the deep, dark, and dangerous ocean, never to be seen again.

The audience was silent, but they suddenly went wild. A massive wave had suddenly appeared and engulfed Tidalus. That was no natural phenomenon. Some audience members, suspecting that the gods had done that, fell to their knees and begged to them, in hopes of rescuing Tidalus, but none of their pleas were answered. Calls for rescue boats were sent out, and men went out to look for Tidalus's body.

Days passed without a trace of the missing swimmer, and it was quite obvious that he had passed away, gone down to the Underworld. In honor of him, he was given his own private cemetery. Many of his fans wept as an empty coffin was lowered into the grave.

As for the massive wave, Poseidon named it in honor of Tidalus. Today, it is still known as the tidal wave.

Seasons of Grief

Lara Elliott

She passed in my grip. I had clung to her hand hard as if my presence could bring her back. I choked on the words that swam in my throat, insisting that they needed to be released. She couldn't leave me. There was so much that I needed to say. Somebody's hand touched my shoulder. They expected that a single touch could comfort me, comfort me not only through her death, but through mine too. What was left for me now? The sound of the flatline resonated in my mind. They had turned the sound off before she had died, but I heard it anyway. The sound has been engrained in my mind ever since. The one sound in the otherwise silent room.

My tears fell as I stared at her face. Her face once smiling and bright. Her face that cheered me up and made me laugh no matter what. Her face, now pale and sickly. The softness had drained from her cheeks, leaving the cold and stiff look I saw now.

"She's gone. We are so sorry."

Anger courses through my veins. They had said that to a million other patients. This time was not unique or meaningful to them in any way.

"No, you're not!" I scream. Spit flies from my mouth, but I couldn't care less about how I look to them. They had killed her. There was nothing more to it than that. I can't hold my feelings in any longer.

"This is your fault! She told you not to, but you did anyway! She'd still be here if you'd have listened to her!" Steaming tears fall from my eyes burning trails into my skin. I stand up from my chair, my vision blurred with anger. There wasn't anything I could do for her now, but they, *they* could've done something. Someone reaches for my arm, but I shake it away. The last thing I need is their "compassion." They speak as I leave the room, something about how it was the only thing they could do and I don't understand. But I can't be here anymore. Not with her remains.

I run, faster than I have before. I can't see where I'm going, but it was away from the hospital. A loud screech forces me to stop in my path. I blink away my tears only to see a middle-aged woman sitting in a car. She looks shocked and stares at me for a few seconds. She has a kind face that almost reminds me of her. For a moment I want to run to her and collapse in her arms as she strokes my hair, but it's not her and there never will be anyone that can be her again. The woman reaches for the handle of her car door, but I take off before she can move another muscle.

My lungs burn, but I push harder. The trees around me draw in closer, locking me in a tight embrace. An embrace I need, but not the one I crave. My legs collapse beneath me unable to hold the weight of my body. I suck in the air around me and force the oxygen to fill my lungs. Sharp twigs press into my knees sending shots of pain up my legs. But nothing could be more painful than what I am feeling. I grab a handful of dirt from the ground. The soil wedges itself under my fingernails. I will never be allowed back in the hospital now. But I never want to go back.

The cancer had taken everything from her body. It took and took until nothing but infected cells controlled her being. It was awful to watch; I can't imagine how she had felt. Maybe I could have done more. I could have stayed by her side for longer and held her tighter. My strength might have passed on to her, given her a reason to keep pushing through her sickness. I know I could have done more. It is impossible to accept it, but I know the truth. The question will forever be burned into the back of my mind. What more could I have done?

My throat is raw. My screams barely audible, just an amalgamation of breathy sobs. My head pounds and heart aches. My cheeks are red and puffy, covered by lines my tears have created. I feel sick, a deep pain gnawing at my stomach, begging I let it consume me. I want to. I want it all to stop. I want a single solution for this never-ending problem of my life. But nothing can stop it, and nothing will. If it consumes me, am I not giving it what it wants?

My grief is a disease. It eats at my body until I am nothing more than a shell of myself. My humanity, thoughts, happiness are stripped until there is no hope of finding them again. That's what happens if I give in. I am eaten alive from the inside out. Nothing could be more torturous.

I bury my face in my hands. The dirt from them is transferred to my face, but it feels cool, calming almost. I allow my breathing to slow and pass through my lungs fully. Soon, they are no longer shallow, but deep and consistent, the way they should be. I brush the hair that had stuck to my tears back with my fingers. It is greasy and knotted, the way hers had always been. I gather myself and push up onto my feet. They feel as if a million needles are being stuck into them over and over again, the pounding loud and constant. It travels to my head and makes me want to scream, but I can't. I physically can't. My mouth has been sewn shut by the rawness that presses against my voice, depriving it from much needed moisture.

The pounding recedes and I feel numb. Nothing passes through me; nothing escapes. My legs move before my body; they can take me wherever I need to go. The trees densify and hug me closer, but I don't need their embrace. I see the opening in the trees and then nothing. That's where I belong now. Away from all this mess and disease that riddles my body.

The cliff is steep with jagged edges. I stand at the edge and look down. The edges are cruel and loom toward me in an unwelcoming and taunting manner.

And then, I'm awake. I don't know how I got here or what I'm doing here. The tears are welling in my eyes again. I can't deal with this anymore. I drop to my knees and lay my hands in my lap. There is a valley beneath me covered in lush trees and nature. It is pure and untouched by the sadistic hand of humanity; a kind innocence remains with a tiny touch of hope. It seems silly that just a few trees could provide any sense of hope.

She is gone. She is gone, I can't bring her back, and there's nothing I can do. There was nothing I could have done, and nothing anyone else could have done. She was sick. It was inevitable. It doesn't make it any easier though, but whoever said grief was easy.

I scoot away from the edge of the cliff to separate myself from the drop. I stare out into the valley. The green mass consumes the land in a warm blanket. My tears continue to fall but not with the same fire that they had previously. I'm not okay, and I don't think I will be for a while. But I think, I hope, that one day I will be.

Fate

Meghan Kinkade

It was never supposed to happen like this—I swear it. If only your friends had stayed away, if you hadn't screamed, everything would've gone differently. You only have yourself to blame for this situation.

I'm sorry. That was rude of me.

My name's Jack. Let me tell you my story.

It was a hot August day, the Arizona sun merciless. The poor air conditioning was close to dead, but it chugged on. I was doing the usual: helping Dad make his rounds. The old pickup's bed had two boxes left for delivery. So close to being done, and Dad was talking up a storm with old Mr. Lynch. I waited outside, like always, feet on the dash as I watched the world crawl by through half-lidded eyes.

That's when I saw you. You were with two friends, coming out of the shop across the way. You had your sunglasses holding back your hair—I imagined running my hands through it, how soft it would be. You were laughing at something, your head thrown back and stars in your eyes.

The other girls couldn't hold a candle to you. One of them had her eyes glued to her phone. How she could be distracted in your presence, I had no idea. The other had your looks—same bright eyes, tanned skin, and light hair—but on her, they just looked wrong.

As you crossed the street, I leaned to the side unconsciously. *Creak!* My support disappeared. I tumbled out of the truck, palms stinging against the ground. Dad stood there awkwardly, clutching the car door. He couldn't meet my furious gaze. "Sorry, son."

My fists clenched, heart racing. *How dare he make a fool of me in front of you!* The anger boiled inside of me until I thought I might burst. You would hate me now. I'd forever just be that idiot who fell out of the car. Even worse, you might laugh, but it would be all twisted—a cruel, pointed thing that jabbed at me.

A pair of white sandals stopped in front of me. A feather-light touch grazed my shoulder—your hair brushing me as you held out your hand. Do you remember that? Your beautiful hand, the one with the light blue nails and the stacked charm bracelets touched *me*. "Are you okay?" you asked, your voice as soft as your hair.

I couldn't even answer as your hand gripped mine—a perfect fit. Your friend scoffed at me from over her phone. Heat rose in me again, but you stroked a tiny circle on my palm, instantly dousing the fire. "I'm Elena," you said, tugging at your hand.

"Elena," I repeated, savoring the feel of it in my mouth. I instinctively gripped harder, still star-struck. I memorized every detail of your face, from your dimples to the tiny scar at your hairline. *You must not recognize me,* I realized. No one from my school—or even my neighborhood—would dare come close. Your friend seemed to get the message, but why didn't you?

"Come on," whined the other girl—your sister—pulling at your other arm.

Your smile slowly melted as you stared at our hands. Something flickered in your eyes—realization. You knew as well as I that we were meant to be together. When you opened those glossy pink lips, I tensed, thinking you finally recognized me. Instead, you cracked a smile. "Can I have my hand back?"

Some emotion filled me—not embarrassment—disgust. Yes. And anger. Disgust that you were so unfairly captivating. The anger was for your greedy sister, trying to hoard you all to herself. The other girl was no better. If you didn't recognize me, she surely did. It was only a matter of time before she told you of Creepy Jack, Four-Eyes Jack.

"I—uh—sorry," I muttered, releasing your hand. I turned

away, ready to flee home. I could forget about you because surely you'd do the same for me.

"Come on, Elena, Jaime," your friend with the phone called. Together, they pulled you away from me. In that instant, I could have killed them.

"Have a nice day," you called, offering me a tiny wave.

A new feeling settled in my heart, growing for every mile we drove away from you. It was determination. Some would even say fate. I would see you again, and I would make you mine. If you didn't understand, you'd see. I'd show you. You and those friends of yours.

It had been nearly a year and a half since then. I hadn't seen you since. You probably forgot all about me, but I needed to see you again.

Normally, social media meant more torment, yet I couldn't live without it. I forced Dad to get me a phone. We didn't have much money, but I *needed* it. The glimpses of you that I got through your friends' accounts were enough. It made every "Jelly Legs Jack" taunt bearable.

I absorbed every bit of info I could on you. Age seventeen, Libra, allergic to dogs, likes pop music, and the junior class president of St. Agatha's. You truly didn't know me then. I could have a fresh start. There was no better chance to do that than the Winter Dance.

For the first time in my life, I began to obsess over my appearance. My glasses? Swapped them for contacts. My hair? Too unruly, too long. My clothes could stay, but I needed something special.

This is why people had friends, I decided as I held up two pink ties next to a suit jacket. I had no experience in this area. Dad was no better. When I mentioned that I was going suit shopping, he just grunted. "We don't have that much money."

"I'm going to the dance with someone, Dad."

He grunted again, glassy eyes staring at the TV. "It's about time you got a friend."

The volcano exploded. I lashed out, smashing a glass against the wall. Blood ran down my palm—the one you had touched. It was Dad's fault. If he hadn't made me angry—

"She's my date," I growled, stomping off. When I finally came back downstairs, more empty beer bottles had appeared. Dad was nowhere to be seen, but a wrinkled stack of twenties sat on the counter.

Only $80? Did he want me to look like a fool?

I stroked the printed picture of you that I kept taped to the dash. It was slightly torn in the corner—Dad would pay for that later—but your smile was enough to keep me sane. I fixed my hair, imagining your arms around me. *Soon enough.*

That night, I waited patiently in the chilled air outside the school. You were going; your friend's Instagram confirmed that. Moments later, I saw you: a goddess with your hair all pinned up. Your dress was pink, my tie matching. *See? Fate.*

Your friends surrounded you, and I never hated them more than in that moment. When your date wrapped his arm around you, I just about lost it. You were *mine*! It should be *my* hand playing with the sash around your waist, not his! He didn't deserve you. None of them did.

It wasn't my fault. You must realize this. The way you two danced together, the constellations in your eyes, focused only on him. How you nestled your head into his shoulder and laughed at his dumb jokes, rubbing his palm the way you did mine—

It was too easy. He deserved it. *No, don't cry. Listen to me.* You went to the bathroom; he met up with your sister, Jaime. The two wove through the crowd, sneaking out the side door. I followed—naturally—my hand going to my pocket. I came prepared. I needed to protect you.

The two walked hand in hand down the sidewalk,

teetering slightly. She had a flask in her hand; he was still holding your purse in his—*your* purse, that *you* had touched. He still gripped it tight as he kissed her—

Traitor. Cheater. Liar. Just like the rest of them.

Heat scorched my veins, a red haze descending over my eyes. I didn't realize what happened until you screamed. (When did you get here?) I didn't know how the knife got into my one hand, your purse in the other, how bloodstained my hands and my clothes were. Two still bodies and a river of red, but I had never felt so powerful.

The way you looked at me...like I was a monster when I was just protecting you. The horror and disgust were written all over your face as you reached for your phone, face paling as I crushed it under my heel. It pained me to destroy something of yours, but it was necessary.

This was their fault. Theirs and yours. I'd never hurt you, but you still put up a fight. You tried to run, but your heel caught in the sidewalk. *Snap!* You crashed to the ground.

I carried you all the way to the car, wishing I could incinerate the ground that dare hurt you. I set you in the back seat and drove here as sirens rushed past. Now no one would come between us.

You need to know. It was all for your own good. I needed to make you understand before you called the cops and ruined everything.

We belong together.

Seeing without Sight

Anika Noby Moolan

The screaming had been going on for almost five hours now.

It was like a game of tug-of-war: both sides going back and forth, each fighting to gain the upper hand. On one side, there was the confident, booming voice of a police officer. That was my dad. On the other side, there was a younger voice, full of the same passion and anger as my dad's voice. That was my oldest brother Evan.

The argument had begun even before Randy, my other older brother, and I had returned home from school. For us, it was supposed to be just another normal day. Like at the end of every other school day, all the other kids ran off, and I waited at the school building for Randy to come walk me home. That's just how life works when you're blind, like me.

The day stopped being normal when we stepped inside our house to hear a familiar yet unexpected voice. Evan was home. Our older brother Evan, the same Evan who had left home before he had even turned eighteen, who only occasionally visited for me and Randy, who hadn't spoken to my dad in five years, was now standing in the living room.

Before we heard anything, our mom had ushered me and Randy up to our rooms, almost as if trying to shield us from the palpable hostility downstairs. But I knew what was going on. It felt just like the day Evan had left in the first place: August 2,1956, just two days before Evan's eighteenth birthday. That day, there had been a lot of arguing and door-slamming, which had all ended with Evan coming upstairs to say goodbye to me and Randy. The overwhelming feeling of déjà vu that I felt now told me that Evan and my dad were arguing about the same thing that had made Evan leave home in the first place: segregation.

I had never really understood segregation, not because I was too young or too ignorant, but simply because I couldn't understand what color was. Being blind, I didn't know what it meant to be light-skinned or dark-skinned, to be "white" or "colored." All I knew was that it made a big difference. Whether you were "white" or "colored" practically decided where you could go and what you could do. My parents told me that the "colored" people were bad for us, the "white" people, and that it would just benefit everyone if we all just kept our lives separate. But Evan didn't agree with them. That was why he had left home.

When Evan said goodbye that day, I asked him why he was leaving. Despite it being five years ago, I still remember his exact answer.

"Rebecca, there are some people in this world, like our parents, who believe that looks reflect who a person truly is. But that's not true. I know that you don't understand me now, and maybe you never will, but always remember that a person is defined by their heart."

His response had simply confused me even more. Though I never told anyone, it occasionally plagued me, not being able to understand segregation, which was such a fundamental part of our society. It made me feel lost, like I would never be able to understand the world around me, just because I couldn't see. A small part of me still wonders whether Evan was right about it all. When that little feeling tries to break through, I try to remember how many people, including my own parents, support segregation, and that helps me push it all away.

***

Two months after the "incident," summer vacation started. With my best friend being out of town all summer, there wasn't much for me to do, especially since I spent a lot of the day home alone.

It was monotonous, staying alone day after day. Every passing minute felt like an hour, and each of those minutes was yet another where I felt trapped in my own mind, with nobody to talk to and nothing to do.

Sometime during the second week of vacation, I was sitting in the backyard when I heard laughter, and not just any laughter, but kids' laughter. But the laughter wasn't coming from our neighborhood. It was coming from the thick group of trees behind our backyard.

I had to go. If I didn't go back there, I could miss out on a chance to find a new friend, someone to talk to during the seemingly never-ending days. So, I cautiously started hurrying toward the now dying laughter.

Right when it seemed like I had reached an open space, I tripped over a large root on the ground and tumbled onto some rough pavement.

Tears pricked at my eyes as a result of the stinging pain in my leg. For a while, it seemed like there was nobody there, like there was no point in even calling out. But suddenly, when I had given up all hope, a pair of strong hands lifted me off the ground.

"You good?" The voice was definitely that of an older teenager. "My name's Elliot," he said, and I guessed that he was sticking out his hand, waiting for me to shake it.

"I'm Rebecca. If you're sticking out your hand for me to shake, I can't see it. I'm blind," I blurted out.

"Oh. Well, okay then. Listen, I'm gonna sit you right here while I go get my sister. She's around your age, and she's real good at patching people up." Elliot set me down on the curb, and I heard the light thumps of his sneakers hitting the ground as he ran the other way.

I sat there for what seemed like an eternity, and I was starting to wonder whether Elliot had abandoned me on the street when a girl's voice cut through the silence.

"Hey, I'm Dawn." She sat down beside me. "That's a pretty bad scrape on your knee. Let me put some medicine on it." Before I could even respond, she was already pouring out some medicine. "So, you're Rebecca, right? What were you doing here?" she asked pleasantly.

I was starting to wonder where exactly "here" was when I felt the sting of medicine being pressed against my leg.

"It's not that bad, right?" Dawn's quirky yet concerned voice cut through the pain. And somehow, despite everything that had just happened, I felt like I would come back, just to befriend this kind and helpful stranger.

***

It was one of the last days of vacation. My little feeling had been right. Dawn and I had become fast friends, and my boredom had been relieved. Today, Dawn and I sat on the pavement, talking and laughing.

But suddenly, out of nowhere, the sharp sound of police sirens filled the air.

"Elliot!"

The sirens had subsided, but Dawn suddenly screamed for her brother and ran away. I was confused. What had scared Dawn so badly? Was Elliot okay?

Suddenly, a gunshot rang out. That was when I heard her scream, louder than anyone I'd ever heard before. Then, another shot rang out, and the screaming stopped.

A part of me knew before it even registered in my brain. "DAWN!" I screamed, praying for a response. "DAWN!"

"Rebecca? What are you doing here?" It wasn't Dawn's voice that responded. It was my dad's. Instinctively, I ran toward his voice.

"Dad! My friend, Dawn, she ran toward the shots! You have to help!" A small part of me wondered what my dad was doing here, but I brushed off the uncertainty and hurried to him.

"Rebecca, why are you here? This is a colored neighborhood!" My dad seemed too shocked to hear my questions and screams. His words suddenly registered in my brain.

"What?" I asked. My head swam. If this was a "colored" neighborhood, that meant…that meant that Dawn was "colored" too. "That's n-not true," I sputtered in disbelief. Dawn wasn't bad at heart. She didn't want terrible things for me or anybody else. She was just the opposite: caring, hilarious, and intelligent.

That was when it all clicked. The police sirens, Elliot, Dawn running to him, the gunshots, and my dad, a cop. Slowly, taking deep breaths, I turned to my dad and asked, "Why are you here?"

"I was here investigating a suspect in the convenience store robbery downtown. His name was Eli or Leott or something. We tried to apprehend him, but he kept insisting that he was innocent and wouldn't cooperate with us. There were shots fired, and some girl ran into it all." His voice was cold and indifferent, as if this was all just routine for him.

"WHAT HAVE YOU DONE?" I screamed. "THEY WERE GOOD, INNOCENT KIDS! AND YOU GUYS JUST SHOT THEM!" Suddenly, a worse thought popped into my head. "WAS IT BECAUSE HE WAS COLORED? DID YOU EVEN HAVE PROOF THAT HE WAS GUILTY? DID YOU EVEN TRY TO LISTEN TO HIM? OR DID YOU JUST ASSUME THAT HE WAS BAD, JUST BECAUSE HE DIDN'T LOOK LIKE YOU?"

Everything that I had once known was quickly crumbling. My thoughts swirled around my mind, just out of reach. Everything was a big blur, and all I could recognize was betrayal and despair. It felt like my identity was falling apart, like there wasn't a single part of me that I could hold on to.

But suddenly, that little feeling, the one that had always told me that Evan was right about it all, that feeling finally broke through. I finally understood. I understood segregation and how wrong it was. I realized that injustice is everywhere, and that it was up to good people to stop it. And for the first time, I could finally see.

Rubies

Hasmik Tumasyan

Prince Lucas was blindly loved by all. He was loved by lovers and children, warriors and scholars, nobility and peasants. Hell, he was even loved by the dragons he had slaughtered. Above all though, he was loved by the rubies that shone so proudly in his room. Lucas had a rock collection as a child, and his mother had told him to stop being a filthy peasant and gifted him a handful of rubies instead. He didn't know what that meant. He was just pleased that they were shiny.

When Lucas was a boy, his father had told him to be just like the rubies. Proud, sturdy, and most of all, charming. The king, of course, was a crazy old man, but still, Lucas grew up alongside the rubies. He held his head up high when he walked. He never ran away from a fight. He kept his sleek black hair perfectly groomed, and his face clean-shaven. His father was proud of his son, the perfect reflection of the old king's years in boyhood. Lucas hated almost everything he forced himself to do. He hated swordsmanship. He was bad at it. His father told him no woman would fall for a man who didn't know how to protect her. He covered it up by tripling all his efforts.

Be like the rubies, he thought. *Proud, sturdy, charming.*

Eva was also blindly loved by all. She was loved by the men in the kingdom who tripped over themselves trying to win her hand. She was loved by her mother and father who tripped over themselves trying to marry her off. She was DEFINITELY loved by the dragons who adored carrying her off into obscure towers to be saved by obnoxious "heroes." She also was loved by the myriad of rubies given to her by rich young suitors. When Eva was a girl, her mother had told her to count the rubies on the king's crown. Eva drew meaning from them. She decided they meant wealth, silence, and most of all, beauty. Eva grew up alongside the rubies. She displayed her family's wealth in the form of a diamond brooch on her dresses. She never spoke unless spoken to. She kept her chestnut hair perfectly brushed, and her clothing stainless. Her mother was proud of her daughter, so independent yet beautiful. Eva hated almost everything about her life. She hated not being able to speak. She was fairly loud. She tripled all her efforts, though. She dared not anger her mother.

Be like the rubies, she thought. *Wealthy, silent, beautiful.*

As the young, charming prince of the kingdom, Lucas had to fulfill his duty of slaying dragons and rescuing pretty girls from towers. It was a tiresome job, but Prince Lucas adored the thrill of his work. At least, that's what everyone thought. In reality, it wasn't that great. It was dangerous and rather annoying actually. Sometimes he would curse to himself atop his steed, wondering if these women WANTED to be abducted. Which, honestly, they most likely did. Each time, the old king would always tell him to marry one of the damsels he had saved, and each time he would make excuses. After all, it wasn't the girls he liked; it was the admiration. The girls didn't matter. They were mere figureheads atop his horse, saddle-warmers. It became a sort of game for him, to see what stupid excuse his father would buy.

This particular time though, Lucas had enough. His breath was an angry spirit in his chest as he gripped the reins on his horse. Lucas promised himself that this would be the last time he would do this. It wouldn't be that hard, after all; he was used to it. Just kill the damn dragon, get the girl, and get out of there. Done, that would be it. Last dragon, last girl, last melodramatic ride into the sunset. All his life he'd been doing exactly what his father told him to. But this time, that old man would just have to deal with it. Lucas arrived at the tower where some lady was being held captive.

One last time, he thought. *Proud, sturdy, charming.*

"I have come to save you, fair maiden!"

Eva frantically rushed to the window of the tower upon hearing Lucas's booming voice. She looked down at him, entranced. He looked almost like a painting, his sword brandished, his snowy white horse below him.

What a surprise, she thought.

Eva was just taking her sweet time, enjoying this gray brick tower her parents told her to stay in, looking "as helpless as possible," when the kingdom's very own pride and joy, Prince Lucas, came to rescue her! Now she understood the absolute genius of her mother's command. Of course, they were going to marry her off to the prince! All of these thoughts, however, were as forced as they could come. Eva tried to be excited. It didn't work. Honestly, she just felt annoyed at her parents for such a downright stupid and extravagant ploy. Of course, she had been abducted by dragons before in the past—she wasn't an amateur! But to be deliberately led to a tower? Truly, this was something else.

"Do you have any rubies?" Eva called down to the young prince. It was a bit dumb, but she awaited the rush that she so commonly associated with the rubies her suitors gave her. Maybe if she saw the glimmering red gemstones once again, it would evoke some feelings for Lucas.

"Excuse me?"

"You've got to have *some*, right? You're like…the king's son."

"Well, y-yes but not on hand. I—just—where's the dragon?" Lucas stumbled on his words. What was this girl saying? In a way though, this was kind of refreshing. Lucas never had long conversations with the women in the towers.

He found himself wanting to hear her ramble more about rubies or whatever she was talking about.

"I don't know."

"What do you mean you don't know? Why are you even up here then?"

"I mean, my family certainly has the budget to afford a dragon. I wouldn't be surprised if one flew over our heads right now," Eva remarked nonchalantly. "So, you're a prince?"

"You know, I'm kinda on a horse, screaming about dragons, and here to rescue you from a tower. What else would I be, a fishmonger?" Lucas didn't remember the last time he made a joke for the sake of making a joke. He didn't know what this woman was doing to him. He didn't get a laugh. It didn't matter though.

Lucas felt free. Eva and Lucas stayed there for what seemed to be hours. Their conversation was very awkward actually, but both sides enjoyed it. It felt sort of forbidden for Lucas. He wasn't acting proud, sturdy, and certainly not charming. They were simply talking to one another. They talked about their families, their suitors, and those godforsaken rubies. It was a strange sight, a prince and a damsel speaking to each other about domestic life and other such insignificant topics. Eventually, Lucas noticed the sun starting to set. It was time to leave. It would be inconvenient to ride through the dark. With any other woman, he wouldn't care. But Eva wasn't a figurehead, a saddle-warmer. She was his friend now.

Eva was happy. She was happy when they talked, and she was happy riding with Lucas into the sunset. The ride wasn't anything to write home about, at least from an outsider's perspective. It was bumpy, awkward, like any interaction they had. They just kinda...sat there, bumping into each other the entire time. She knew her mother would think that she was stupid. She always taught her that women were friends and men were suitors. But she didn't see Lucas as a suitor, and she was sure he didn't think of her as someone he would court. She looked to the sky, red like rubies, a silent reminder of the uncertainty of the near future. It reminded Eva that she would have to rethink everything she was told. But she didn't at that moment.

Lucas and Eva knew that when they arrived back to the kingdom they would have to face their parents and their lives. They knew they would likely never see each other again, but it didn't matter. The evening was filled with banter, growing more enthusiastic and smooth as time went on. As the gates of the kingdom came into view, uncertainty struck their hearts. It was only a matter of time until Lucas had to make another excuse and Eva would perhaps follow suit. Maybe they would fight with their parents; maybe they wouldn't. But they would never forget each other, and they would most CERTAINLY toss out those rubies.

Colors

Ayala Erez

Red

It's what you see when your eyes first land on her. It's what is blossoming in your chest as you dance the night away. It is the color of her lips as she beckons you closer. It's the mark you want to leave on her after the night is over. It's what you feel, see, and become as you fall more in love… It's the whistle in your ears when you see her in bed with another. It's the vase now broken on the floor in your anger. It's the blood running from the physical cuts on your hand and the emotional cuts in your heart. It's the words streaming out of your mouth as she apologizes for cheating. It's the feeling and moment of when you drive away in tears and heartbreak. It's red, it's anger, it's passion, and it's love.

Orange

It's in the way she flips her hair, a little too seductively. It's the beat of your heart when she pulls out the chair across from you, not in love, but definitely curious. It's the rumbling of your stomach and the laugh she produces because of it. It's the warm coffee and smiles that aren't quite familiar, but you want them to be. It's the sound of nothing as the sunset leaves and you're enveloped in darkness, with her in your arms… It's the distasteful feeling in the air as she leaves for the army. It's the leaves that fall as you pass, your longing for her becoming theirs. It's the flag you get, and it's the knowledge she'll never come back. It's not the tears. It's the loneliness as you watch the sunset without her in your arms. It's orange, it's powerful, it's confusing, and it's lonely and noticeable when darkness overtakes it.

Yellow

It's her smile as you lift her in a field of sunflowers. It's the feeling you get when you hear her laugh. It's the sound you hear when your down on one knee and she says yes. It's the blessed feeling of planning and preparing to spend the rest of life doing everything together. It's standing at the altar waiting for your love to arrive… It's the light that leaves you when she never comes. It's the energy that falls from your eyes as tears and leaves your soul when it dawns upon you that she never loved you. It's yellow, it's happiness, it's laughter, and it's gone when the fun's over.

Green

It's the warmth when you step outside at dawn. It's the freshness of the lemonade she pours for you. It's the breeze in her hair and dress as she practically floats away. It's the carefree feeling and easygoing nature of the situation when you give her your number. It's the smoothness of your shirt on the first date. It's the sweet feeling of being on top of the world when you're near her. It's the sourness in the air when you cry to the gods, wondering why she left you. It's the plants wilting in the earth as you desperately try to revive them and make yourself forget her. It's the damp mood when you remember she dumped you over text. It's the messages sent to your friends bashing her looks, personality, and choices. It's green, it's cool, it's fresh, and it can get dark when the sun leaves.

Blue

It's her tears when you first see her. It's the sound of your heart breaking because you hate to see her in pain. It's the wind when you calm her down, soft and smooth. It's the beating of your heart as she hugs and thanks you. It's the breathtaking view when she comes in looking stunning on your first date. It's the words that leave your mouth that make her fall in love with you. It's the messy hair and sweet smiles when waking up next to her… It's the tears running down when she leaves you. It's the baths running and self-care days attempting to remove the pain. It's the hookups you had out of remorse from losing her. It's the sad feeling in the air that you breathe without her there. It's blue, it's calm, it's sweet, and it's tears.

Purple

It's the sereneness of the flowers in the wind. It's the smile when she bounces over to your blanket on the grass, her smile calm and nice, like nothing wrong is possible. It's the movement of the clouds as you cloud-watch on what appears to be your first date with her. It's the softness of her touch as you tickle each other and laugh all night. It's the look in her eyes when she really looks at you. It's the aura coming from her, deep and dark, when she is forbidden from seeing you again. It's the knowledge in your soul that you belong together. It's the wind that passes by as her train leaves the station, mad and ominous. It's the darkness that arises, not quite black, but as close as it can get. It's the cries in the midst of the hurricane of life. It's purple, it's calm, it's sweet, and it's the worst part of the storm when things don't go the way that's wanted.

Beauty at Sea

Nya Benoit

I sat yet again, another morning looking upon the rolling hills of the horizon. The weather was soft and thick, a bit humid this evening. I stuck my old, wrinkled finger into the air, feeling the wind against my skin. The air was salty and crisp against my face. I closed my tired eyes tightly, as the wind grazed over me almost as if it were planting soft, chilly kisses against the top of my head and creeping down my spine. The familiar feeling triggered something inside of me. Something that I thought I was too old to remember. But how could I ever forget.

It was 1962, and I was stationed in San Diego. A young man I was, young indeed. Nineteen years young I believe to be exact. Didn't have much knowledge about the world or the people around me. All I knew was that there was a great enemy and to do what I was told. But most importantly I knew that I was doing a great deed for my country. I had much pride in knowing this.

"Are ya coming, Scott?" I had a comrade that I had considered to be a very close friend. Fred McCartney. Fred was twenty-three and knew more about the world than I did. He would often tell me stories about his life before he was drafted. Usually they consisted of him being drunk or a girl or two. I valued these stories. My father was a drunk, and my mother was a weak, small woman. Even though I was a young man, I lacked a lot of my own experiences because of the way I had been raised.

"Yeah. Freddy, I'm coming right along."

There was a pub up along the shore all the men were going to. Little did I know that the Old Town Saloon would soon become one of the most memorable places in all my years that

I would ever experience. That old dusty salon is where I met her.

Fred and I walked in just as she took her place sitting in a small booth filled with luminous light from the lamp dangling above her. I wasn't the only one who had noticed her. Other men in uniform were whispering about, hesitant to make their presence known. I had taken my place at the bar, nervous. She was only a few feet away. Fred was ordering us beers, and it was the perfect time for me to sneak a peek at her. I glanced over, and my poor young heart skipped beats to find that she was already looking at me. Her face was heart-shaped and delicate, and her soft brown hair framed her face perfectly. Her skin looked like porcelain and gleamed underneath the luminescence that hung above her. But her eyes. Her eyes made me feel something so intense; I had yet to feel anything like it. Looking at them, I felt as though I was lost at sea, sinking. Struggling to slice my way through the water, desperate to inhale. Her eyes were the light, the light teasing me above the water giving me hope that being six feet underwater would not faze me to reach my freedom.

"She sure is a looker, Scott."

And just like that, the trance was broken.

"Huh. Oh yeah. She is."

"Ya think I got a shot?" Fred took a swig of his beer and adjusted his patrol cap.

"Now, Freddy, you know good and well if anyone could, it would be you." I gave him a weak, halfhearted smile for encouragement.

"That's why you're the best, Scott." And he skipped his way over toward her without another word.

I looked down into the darkness of my own beer. Looking into my reflection I sighed, desperately wishing I was the one talking to the beauty in the booth.

"Come on, guys," a deep, gruff voice boomed behind me

followed by an echo of heavy footsteps.

I looked over and watched as Greg Hartley and three other men made their way toward Fred and the mystery girl.

"Hey there, darlin'," Greg said, interrupting Fred, who was trying to muster up a conversation. "How about you and that pretty face of yours comes and sits with us real men at that booth over there."

She flashed a big, white, mischievous smile. "Uh." She glanced over at me as I watched for her response. She was making me dizzy again. Her expression seemed almost as though she was asking me for help.

"Actually, there, Greg," Fred started. "We were just talking..."

"I don't give a damn what you were just doing, McCartney," Greg said, his voice rising.

The tension began to rise as well. I made my way over, knowing Fred would sooner rather than later say something he shouldn't, digging himself into even more trouble.

"Let's not start something we shouldn't finish," I said, making my presence known.

Greg's and Fred's eyes did not dare break contact. I looked down at the sweet girl. Her lips parted slightly, and her eyes darted back and forth between the two rivals.

"Actually, Gregory, I think a damn best be exactly what you give."

And just like that, the first gunshot was fired.

Punches were thrown and glasses were shattered. Soon, there was a red sea of drunk, bloody men trying to dominate one another. But the only thing I was worried about was the poor, gorgeous girl witnessing it all. Fred and Greg tackled each other to the floor, smashing each other with beer bottles and pinning each other down hoping to outweigh the other.

Without thinking, I grabbed the girl's hand and sought my

way out. I felt her swiftly follow behind me. She squeezed my hand a little tighter the closer we got to the door.

"Scott!"

My neck snapped in the direction toward the crowd. Greg's face slowly came into view. "Where do you think you're going?"

I looked at her. She slowly shook her head no, telling me not to dare to go back in there. I looked and saw Fred. My first real friend on the floor, bleeding out from a gash deep in his forehead.

"Go," I said to her. "Meet me on the beach in an hour."

I pushed her out the door, dove into the crowd, and saved my best friend.

Now, I'm too old to remember details. But even so it was quite a blur. The last thing I remember is dragging Fred toward the exit. Barely making it out of the storming pub brawl. The beach was near. I could hear the waves crashing against the rocks that decorated the shoreline. The wind whistled through palm tree leaves, singing to me. I quickly remembered the arrangements I made.

"Scott, I'm all right." Fred chuckled, coughing a bit. "Hey, whatever happened to the girl?" Fred began to pick up his own weight, walking on his own.

"I, uh, I escorted her out."

Fred stretched, whipping the blood from his brow. "Ah. I see."

I looked out into sea. The sun started to set. "Go on, Scotty. I'll make my way back."

"No, Fred. You're injured. I'll walk you back."

Fred got up. He looked out into the sea and pointed. "I'll be okay. And besides, you shouldn't keep her waiting."

I raced toward the beach, holding on to my cap to keep it from flying away. I ripped my boots off once I reached the sand and ran toward her, slowing down the closer I got. She was facing the ocean. She was so close I could smell the lavender scent coming from her hair. My heart seemed to grow larger the longer I stood in her presence. The waves began to steady, and water seemed to still. She turned around, her enticing eyes once again meeting mine.

"Hello," she said to me with a smile. "My name is Anne. What's yours?"

The years went by. I was stationed in other parts of the world near other beaches, but never met a soul as beautiful as hers. She became a part of me. It feels as though the older I become, the stronger that memory lingered within me.

It was now dark outside. My light from my porch kicked on, telling me it was finally time for me to return inside. My old bones clenched as I rose from my chair, getting ready to go in. I reached my front door and inhaled the deep-sea air. I exhaled softly.

Later, I crawled into bed, closed my eyes, and whispered "Good night" to my beauty at sea.

Not My Fault

Nishta Nandakumar

She took a shaky breath as she pulled out the stick from her backpack, which was stuffed with binders and notes from her classes. She paled as the stick revealed her worst fears. Two little lines, staring up at her as she stared down at them, tears filling her eyes. All she heard was a roaring in her ears as her hand slackened and the stick fell out of her grip.

Not your fault, not your fault, she kept telling herself. She knew that it was true. This wasn't her fault. But then, that little voice in her head spoke again. *Maybe it was your fault*, it said. And alas, she began to listen to that voice, zero in on it, drowning out any others. Like the way she felt when she saw the stick. Like the way she felt that night.

She could barely see him; only the silhouette of his face was seen in the dim lights of the house party. The only thing she saw of him were his piercing blue eyes, so cold that she shivered even in the heat of the room. But she felt his touch. Everywhere he touched her, her body seemed to scream in agony. She wanted to scream too. But every time she opened her mouth, no sounds came out. She knew that she said "no" many times that night, timid and pained, barely getting the words out of her mouth. She also knew that no matter what she had said that night, he never stopped. He didn't stop when he saw the tears on her face, the pain in her eyes. He treated her as if she was a piece of meat; like she didn't deserve to be treated as a human being. He didn't stop until he was done. And then he shoved her away and went back to the party as if nothing had happened. As if she was nothing.

She had one drink. One drink had led to *this.* Even though it wasn't enough for her to be completely disoriented, it was enough to weaken her. And he had latched onto that weakness. Just like his hand latched onto her skirt and his mouth latched onto hers.

On that night, she vowed to never drink again.

Now, it seemed as if she wouldn't anyway, for the next nine months at least. She leaned against the wall of her bedroom and fell clumsily to the ground, knocking the papers on the ground everywhere. Then she picked the stick up again with shaky hands. Her eyes kept checking the stick every few seconds, as if by some miracle the results would change. Her hand absentmindedly drifted to her abdomen, settling there in shock.

Not your fault, not your fault, she repeated again and again, like a mantra. But the roaring in her ears grew. It drowned the voice of reason out. She was…going to be a mother. And if she had this child…every single time she saw her child's face, that night would flash before her eyes. She didn't know if she could love her child the way every child deserved to be loved when she saw his face in her child's face every day. She didn't know if she could handle that.

Even worse, she had to see him every day. Every single day. He passed her in the hallways, laughing and slinging an arm around his friends' shoulders. And every single day, she hunched her own shoulders to hide herself from him. His eyes seem to pointedly avoid hers. Was he so intoxicated that night that he didn't even remember what he did and the pain he caused her? Or was he willfully ignoring her, knowingly letting her go through this inner turmoil by herself? She couldn't decide which was worse. Either way it was clear that, to him, she was nothing. She wished she could forget him and his face as quickly as he had forgotten her and her body.

And what would having this baby do to her future? Her grades, college, her future career? Having this baby would have to mean that the baby would take priority. Could she really handle that? She had worked for so much in her life. All through high school, she had been known as the quiet, soft-spoken girl who always got good grades. Where was all of that going to go now? She didn't want people to look at her and assume anything. Like she had assumed when she saw other teen moms—how little they must've cared about their future to let something like that happen! She never even thought that something could've happened to them like it happened to her.

Her body was racked with loud sobs. How was this fair? Why did she have to pay so much for something she never wanted to happen?

Not your fault, not your fault...

Not your fault...

It might not have been her fault. But she was the one who had to deal with this. She curled into herself, shaking. She knew that the father of her baby would currently be out partying with his girlfriend, maybe leaving another girl to the same fate as her. She knew she should tell someone, anyone. But she didn't want to be hated. She didn't want to be pitied. She didn't want to put herself in a worse position for him to make her life more miserable or do the same thing again to her. Because once was one time too much.

Right after he left her on the floor that night, sobbing and disoriented, she knew that she would have to keep this buried inside her. No one should be allowed to know. She didn't want anyone else to think lower of her than she already thought of herself.

She knew she should listen to the voice of reason in her head. She should tell someone, anyone. Then she could share this burden. Then she could feel light for the first time since that night. She could feel as though it wasn't her fault.

Would that really help her? Or would it just break her even further, by having the guilt of forcefully sharing her burden with others on her conscience?

But maybe listening to that voice of reason was a good idea. Then she could take control of some small part of her life. That one night wouldn't have to be hidden deep inside her. There could be someone who she could confide in. She wouldn't feel as alone.

But who would she tell? She couldn't tell her friends—she was too afraid of being judged by them. And anyway, she didn't have any friends anymore, or anyone at school who really cared about her. All of her so-called friends had left her when she started behaving differently, without a care that she might be breaking inside. She couldn't bear to tell her parents either, because she couldn't stand it when they were disappointed in her. And she knew they would be extremely disappointed if they knew their high school daughter was pregnant.

Through her inner turmoil, she vaguely heard her bedroom door creak open. She looked up as a blurry figure of a warm and familiar face appeared before her eyes. She blinked, letting the tears stream down her face farther, waiting for the waves of disappointment and pain to radiate off her mother and slam into her. She didn't even try to hide the evidence. Her mother's face morphed into one of concern, and she saw her mother take in her hand that was still resting on her own abdomen in wonder and pain. She saw her mother register what was in her daughter's hand, and her face blanch as she saw the two little lines. Shock glimmered across her mother's face, turning it a pale white.

She wanted to speak before her mother could make any assumptions. But she couldn't get her words out.

"Mom," she whispered. "He… he…" Her shaky, unstable words were cut off by more sobs and tears streaking down her face. Her mother's eyes flashed with understanding and pain for her only daughter before she was enveloped in a warm, comforting hug.

"It's not your fault, honey. It's not your fault, and it never will be. Don't worry. We'll do something about this." And in the arms of her mother, the only place where she felt safe anymore, she relaxed and morphed back into her younger self, believing every word her mother uttered. She didn't feel as alone anymore.

Not my fault, she thought resolutely, the demons in her mind finally quieting, the roaring finally subsiding.

Not my fault.

Matchmaker

Sarah Wai Kay Tsang

Where is she? A woman stood on the side of the street, wringing her hands in worry. She clutched her phone tightly, waiting. *It's almost time…*

Her thoughts were interrupted by the sound of screeching tires as a car pulled up. A tall woman with a pink-streaked ponytail set high on her head wearing a black pantsuit and red heels stepped out.

"Hi, are you Alyssa?" the woman asked.

Alyssa nodded and the woman smiled.

"Nice to meet you in person. I'm Irene, your dating agent. We spoke over the phone last week. This is your first time meeting Michael, correct?"

Irene glanced at Alyssa expectantly and could tell she was having nervous jitters. "Hey, it'll be all right. I'm here to help. It's my job, and I intend to do it right." She gave her a reassuring smile and a pat on the back. "Okay, your date must be waiting inside. Come on!"

Let's see what we got here... Irene sat down at the next table over from Alyssa and Michael, who had just exchanged greetings.

"Hi, Michael, I hope you don't mind, I hired a dating agent...don't worry though! She isn't going to make this too awkward!" Alyssa said.

Irene nodded. "I'm only here to make sure things go smoothly between you two. I work for a matchmaker company in the dating department."

It was a simple lunch date, nothing too exciting. Alyssa and Michael got to know each other better and were able to sort something out with dates and schedules. They were starting to build a genuine bond. Irene observed everything and took notes. She admired how they were really trying to connect with each other, but she knew that ultimately this relationship was doomed.

By the end of it, the couple confirmed that they wanted to continue seeing each other and were satisfied with how things turned out. As they were heading out of the restaurant, Alyssa turned and thanked Irene for her service. "It was good to know I had a friend with me."

Irene simply smiled. "Anytime! Matchmaker and Company is always at your service!"

Watching them walk away chatting together, Irene glanced at their intertwined hands. *I'd give them about a month, tops.* She couldn't ignore what she saw—the little red strings at the end of their fingers leading in opposite directions.

As she looked up at the bright red lines crisscrossing the sky, connecting everyone to their soul mates, Irene unconsciously rubbed her ring finger, then quickly dropped her hand. All she ever saw when she looked at it was a piece of broken red string dangling at the end of her finger, disconnected, swaying in the wind.

***

The Red Strings of Fate, from the ancient Chinese legends, are said to connect one to their soul mate. Not everyone can see them, but Irene had inherited this ability from her family. As a child, she would often follow the strings from different people just for fun. Her friends in school would tell her who they had a crush on, and she would know whether it was meant to be or not. This ability of hers made her perfect for the job as a dating agent at Matchmaker and Company.

Plopping back down onto her chair in the Matchmaker headquarters, she sighed.

"Hey, Irene!"

"Gah!"

She almost fell out of her chair and looked over her to see her best friend Esme leaning on the table.

"Esme! Can you not sneak up on me like that?"

Esme giggled. "It's great to see you too! How'd the date go? Are they a perfect match?"

Irene couldn't help rolling her eyes at the lame reference to their company's slogan. Esme was the energetic and laid-back type. Sometimes she didn't really take her work seriously at all. These days she was all about being the life of the party.

"Esme, how many times must I tell you to stop causing a ruckus in the office?" Soren said as he walked by with a small stack of folders, papers, and binders. "You should be more focused during work hours—bother Irene once your work is finished."

"Oh, Soren, Soren, Soren—" Esme leaned on his shoulder with her elbow. "You're so uptight. You gotta loosen up every once in a while and relax. Am I right, Irene?" she said, flipping her pale blond hair.

"Maybe…" Irene trailed off, not wanting to continue the conversation. But she couldn't help smiling whenever she saw her two best friends tied by the same red string. She always had to resist the urge to say something. Though tempting, not even her closest friends could know her secret.

"Right, then I'll be getting back to my paperwork."

Soren headed back to his cubicle, leaving Irene to listen to Esme's rambling and gossiping.

"By the way, have you heard anything from your brother? You didn't tell him I liked him, did you?"

Irene gave her a dismissive wave. "No! No, of course not! He's my brother!."

"But Irene!" Esme groaned. "He's just as handsome as you are pretty! And that's saying something! Fine, I won't bring it up." She slumped back into her cubicle but then peeked over the edge at Irene. "Your brother's still hot though."

Irene smacked her on the head.

"Ouch!" Esme sat back down in her chair.

It was only after the sun was setting that Esme came bounding back to Irene to discuss her nonexistent love life. Irene tried to escape, but Esme cornered her in the elevator. Irene moaned and braced herself as soon as her friend opened her mouth.

"You should really try a dating app if no guys have come up to you yet. Your love is out there, and you need to go out and find him!"

Esme was overly dramatic. Irene knew all her talk of "finding true love" wasn't going to happen.

"I told you so many times that's never gonna work. It's just not that simple, and don't forget my parents are really strict. They won't approve of just any guy."

And my red string's broken, dammit.

"Still doesn't hurt to try! Even with strict parents, you should take more control of your life. You're more logical than me. Use that big brain of yours." Esme shrugged.

Irene looked at her friend in exasperation. "You know I'm only focused on my job. It's what I went to college and got my degree for. And why don't *you* have a boyfriend?"

"I just haven't found the right guy yet."

"Then why don't you take your own advice!"

Esme pouted. "Fine. You win. Wanna get dinner?"

Irene shook her head. "Sorry, I promised my family I'd have dinner with them tonight. Let's do it another day."

"All right, see you!" Esme waved goodbye.

Her friend was right though. Irene did think constantly of her love life despite the broken string, but there wasn't anything to be done about it.

At dinner, her mother pressed the topic further, peppering her with questions: "Do you have a boyfriend?" "Are there any nice men at your job?" "Do you like any of them?" "Have you tried dating yet?" "Do you need me to find one for you?" "You know, you should be married before you turn thirty... You're still twenty-seven. There's still time to find a husband and give your father and me grandchildren. The red string doesn't affect who you decide to have a family with."

"Ah, ma! No, I am not dating anyone. I'm not in a rush to get married!" Irene rubbed her forehead and stared down at her steaming bowl of rice.

Her father spoke up. "It's fine if you don't want to get married yet, but you will sooner or later. Look at your brother. He's doing just fine, and he's getting married next year!"

Irene shot a look across the table at her younger brother. She highly doubted that the same guy she had heard complaints about being a playboy would be so willing to commit himself to marriage.

"Oh, come on, sis, just one date," Ian said. "I know a guy you might be interested in. I can set up the date for you." He gave her a knowing smile.

She narrowed her eyes at him, knowing full well he didn't care about what the red strings said. "Look, *bro*, I don't trust you or any of your sketchy friends."

Ian looked up and down at his sister. "You're a professional third wheel aren't you? You should know plenty about dating and how to handle guys."

Irene groaned. "Fine. One date. That's it."

*This was definitely a mistake...*she thought, sitting in a cafe across from her "date." This guy was definitely not someone she wanted to be associated with. Arrogant, self-absorbed, narcissistic...to put it mildly. He talked about himself for more than half an hour, then just got up and left saying he had to "pick up a friend at the airport," one of the lamest excuses in the book.

I shouldn't have listened to my idiot brother, or Esme, or even my parents. Why did I think this would be a good idea? Her downcast expression caught the attention of a nearby waiter who noticed that her date was gone and no one had paid the bill.

"Hey, you doing okay? I'm Leo. Nice to meet you."

Irene looked up at his outstretched hand and saw what she'd only ever seen on herself. A red string hanging from his finger, identical to hers. She didn't know how to think or feel seeing another one like hers, but maybe it was fate, a coincidence, destiny...that gut feeling in her stomach. She smiled and reached out to shake his broken-stringed hand.

"Hi."

Her Vision

Maya Anvar

Nourabad was a small, peaceful village in western Iran. Nature encompassed everything, from the wide, welcoming grassy fields to the rocky mountains looming in the background. Narrow streams crisscrossed between and around the old-fashioned mud houses that blended in with the surrounding nature. Birds chirped, perched in tall trees that held ripe, juicy fruits. They chirped as they drank from little streams. They chirped as they hopped merrily along, and they chirped as they spread their wings and flew in the sky, as free as the wind. The villagers all worked for the community as shepherds and harvesters. Since the village was small, everyone knew each other. Every passerby would know your name and warmly greet you like an old friend.

That is until one harsh summer arrived, taking away the rain and replacing it with a hot, burning sun. The birds stopped singing their joyful songs, and the flowers drooped helplessly, begging for water. All the crops wilted under the blazing sun, which had been mercilessly beating on the village for days on end. Soon enough, the people ran out of water, and with it, their food.

Twelve-year-old Shirine couldn't sleep. She tossed and turned in her bed for hours, but the sleep she longed for never came. Her mouth was dry and her stomach was empty, as it had been for the past thirty-six days. They'd been rationing all the water, grains, and bread they had, to have enough during the rest of the drought, however long it would be.

How long would she survive in this drought? Would she wither away like the crops?

She turned around in bed and twisted up her blankets. Her discomfort made her decide to leave her house to go for a walk in her safe village. In the dark of her house, she slowly and silently walked on her toes so as not to wake her father, sleeping in his room.

Shirine felt like she was gliding as she passed the rows of houses outside and then floating through a nearby farm. That's how night always made her feel—peaceful, tranquil, as if her arms and legs were made of something light and feathery, like wings. She flowed along that way until she reached the foot of the mountain by her village.

Carefully, she grasped a boulder and climbed up, higher and higher, gazing at the endless sky, dotted with stars. She reached a small clearing overlooking a once-flowing waterfall. A gentle wind rustled through the dry grass.

Shirine looked down the mountain to her beloved village, Nourabad, desperately clinging onto life. She looked at the moon, at her kind, motherly face.

"Why must we suffer?" she asked.

The moon didn't answer.

"There is always a reason for everything," her father had told her when her mother left the world. Perhaps her mother had other work to do, elsewhere, he had told eight-year-old Shirine, holding her in his arms as she cried and cried.

"We can't always understand the reason for things, but we must stay strong and have courage no matter what," he had said, tenderly stroking her hair as a tear rolled down his own face.

What could be the reason for the famine? All it brought was despair, death, and emptiness.

Sitting under the moon, wondering, Shirine suddenly heard the faint sound of someone playing the tanbur, a string instrument used for spiritual reflection. Drawn to the celestial, rich sound, she stood and started walking across rocks in the direction of the music. She approached a weeping willow with a curtain of vines hanging down from it, dancing and swaying in the wind.

Shirine gently drew back the vines and gasped. In the middle of a ring of miraculous, fresh grass sat a striking woman in a flowing white gown, her long black hair dancing in the wind to the music of her tanbur. The green grass and flowers circling the woman contrasted with the barren, dry land everywhere else. Her face seemed to glow with a sort of inner radiance.

Not seeming to notice Shirine, she played her music with closed eyes and a blissful expression. Shirine silently edged closer to her and sat at her feet. She closed her eyes and let the music wash over her, feeding her with emotion and light.

Abruptly, the woman stopped playing her tanbur and gazed right into Shirine's eyes. She seemed so familiar, but Shirine could not quite place her. Then the woman spoke.

"Don't worry, Shirine," she said gently. "Your people will survive. A new birth will bring life." The woman stood and walked away without a sound, taking her tanbur with her.

Shirine looked at the place where the woman had been sitting. Where had the fresh grass and flowers gone? All that was left was dry soil. Perhaps—perhaps she had just *imagined* the woman. Perhaps her hunger and thirst had made her see things.

Dazed, Shirine hurried home, wondering about what had happened. It *couldn't* have been true. And yet, it had seemed so real!

"You seem very quiet," remarked Shirine's father the next morning during their daily walk to a field where the last streams of water were.

"Yes," she replied, not caring to explain. What was there to say? She had resolved not to tell anyone about last night's vision. What good would it do except bring false hope?

After seventy-five days of drought, people were in despair. The ruthless sun burned all the crops and killed many farm animals with its wrath. The people all depended on a single stream for water, as all the others had dried up, and this last surviving trickle of water was sure to dry up in the next few days. Many people were on the verge of starvation, and Shirine and her father were no exception. Some people even had to sacrifice their own horses and sheep for meat. As the days grew hotter and drier, the people became more hopeless.

On the eightieth morning of the famine, Shirine awoke and left the house with a dry loaf of bread to give to the old lady, Afsaneh, next door. But what she saw when she went outside was not the famished, miserable village she was expecting to see.

All the streams that were previously dried up were now bubbling with cool, fresh water, and the ground was moist under her feet. There was a refreshing breeze flowing about, and for once, the sun had ceased to beat down upon them. A feathery cloud, like a veil, had finally floated in front of it.

Was this a dream?

All around her, people were coming out of their houses, crying with delight and jumping for joy. Shirine's father came out and put his hand on her shoulder.

Just then, a door opened, and out came Mahtab Khanoom, cradling her newborn baby.

Shirine caught her breath. Could it have been true after all? The woman *had* said that a new birth would save them.

Everyone, including Shirine, crowded around the baby, praising her lovely eyelashes and hazel eyes.

"Her name is Leily," announced Mahtab Khanoom. She let Shirine hold the sweet baby, who had, maybe, just maybe, saved their lives.

Days went by, then months, then years. As Shirine grew, so did Leily. Leily grew into a beautiful young lady who always helped the village with her kindness. When Leily was ten, she found a baby bird drowning in a pond, saved it, and fed it insects and berries throughout the night to keep it alive. At age twelve, she rescued a little boy who was sinking in the mud. For all the acts of kindness Leily continued to perform, the villagers of Nourabad called her the Village Protector.

Leily and Shirine had a very strong bond. As adults they started an organization that sent food to the poor and helped their neighbors through difficult times.

Every year, on the day that the famine had ended, and also the day of Leily's birth, the villagers would have a festival with flowers, food, and music.

On the night of the twentieth anniversary of the end of the famine, Shirine was climbing up the same mountain she had gone to for the first time all those years ago. She had made it a tradition every year to visit the same landmarks.

There was the same boulder she had climbed. And *there* was the same path she had followed to reach the woman she had seen, or imagined seeing. It was all the same, except that the mountain was once again flourishing and bursting with color. The waterfall was back, pouring down with large quantities of water. Shirine followed the path to the weeping willow with the curtain of vines. Now, they were so long that they reached the ground.

Shirine gently pushed aside the vines and stifled a gasp.

The woman was back again! No, it was Leily. No, Leily was the woman. They were the same person!

Leily was sitting in the middle of the clearing, the wind blowing her hair, causing it to float up and down with the breeze. She was holding her tanbur. With closed eyes, as if about to start playing, she had the same serene expression on her face and looked as if she was far away in another world.

"What—how—" Shirine gasped in awe. How had she never realized? She had never connected Leily and the woman in her vision until now.

Leily's eyelids fluttered open, and she answered Shirine's confusion with a smile.

"Shirine, it's time for me to go. You are the new Village Protector. My spirit always knew that you would be my successor." She stood up and kissed Shirine's cheek with sisterly affection. Then, she turned around and walked away, until she disappeared from sight.

Lost Dreams

Maya Anvar

"Why don't some people like to sleep?" asked Emma, turning around in her bed to face me.

I looked down at her from up high in my loft bed. "Because they like to be up and about and awake," I replied. "Like you. You never want to sleep either."

"And maybe they have nightmares and they're scared of having nightmares."

"Well, I like to sleep because I like my dreams."

"Me too," was Emma's response.

After some time, I admitted, "Well…I *used* to, but now...now it's different. I used to have the best dreams about flying. It was a different world in my dreams. It didn't feel at all like this world. I even have different friends there. There's a boy named Peter who loves bananas and a girl named Grace who I met one time in my dream at the Swan Pond. But they're all gone now. And my favorite rock that I practiced flying off! Oh, I miss everything so much. It's been *so* long since I've gone to my dream world. I don't know when I'll fly again, if I ever will."

A great big tear welled in one eye, and I squinted to send that sad, salty tear rolling on its way, down my cheek, down my neck, until it rested on my chest, above my heart. It tickled and felt cold and uncomfortable, but I let it stay.

Was this what happened to all children once they grew up? Did they lose their dreams? Their happiness? Where did the dreams go? Could I ever get them back?

I stared at a glow in the dark star shining on the ceiling. I glared at it. It had no right to be so happy and bright when I was so miserable! I stared at it as I continued to talk, more to myself than to Emma this time.

"Now my dreams are so boring and pointless. Aunt Amelia and I used to always talk about my dreams, but now there won't be anything to talk about when she comes over next week. Sometimes I even have nightmares. And all my dreams are so unimaginative. They're all of *this* world. What did I do for the other lovely half of my life to disappear, melt away? I miss flying. It made me feel so free. And it felt so real all the time. I think it really *was* real. I think it was my soul that was flying all those times in my dreams, not my body. Maybe my soul is trapped here on Earth. Maybe when I was younger, it was free, but over time it was me that trapped it down here. It's my fault. I trapped it here with my faults, by neglecting my imagination, and increasing my devotion to this world and materialistic things, and in general, just growing up."

I had to stop here to catch my breath. I had been talking so fast and intently that I barely had time to breathe. More and more tears were spilling down my cheeks and ending up at my heart.

I couldn't believe that I was pouring out all my grief to my five-year-old sister. I love her, and she is so sweet, but she never really understands me. Well, of course she doesn't. She's just five after all.

"I wish Mary Poppins was here," she said suddenly, interrupting my thoughts. "She's magical. She could make you fly like she did in the movie."

I sighed. Emma didn't understand at all. No one could understand. I was in the depths of despair, and she continued to talk about Mary Poppins as if she was the magical remedy to every problem!

She definitely did *not* understand.

(Aunt Amelia, you would understand. That was when I made a mental note to myself to write this all down in a letter and send it to you. The world needs more aunts like you.)

"Mary Poppins wouldn't make me feel better. She can't take me to my dream world. And besides, she doesn't exist." As I said this, I immediately felt guilty. Here I was, miserable on account of lost dreams, but ruining another's!

(I wish I hadn't said that, Aunty, for you are the one I am writing this for, but since I am recording everything I remember and all my feelings, it is necessary for me to include everything.)

"Well, if you can't fly anymore," Emma pressed on, "you can try to float. Or swim in the air. You can teach yourself in your dreams, right? And you can just teach yourself how to fly all over again. And you can imagine your friends back."

"I guess" was my remark.

But inside I was thinking.

It would never work. I was never able to control anything that happened in my dreams, but I never cared. I loved the unexpected. And they used to always be so pleasant. Besides, I couldn't just bring all my friends back.

I believed they were real. They could come on their own accord. Unless there was some barrier now between my soul and theirs, now that I was growing up.

"Do you remember," I continued, "how much happier I was before I got shut out of my dream world? How much more energetic and cheerful?"

"I think you're still happy, Rosie. You danced to 'Supercalifragilisticexpialidocious' with me today."

"Yes, I try to be very happy, and I often am, but I feel different now. I feel like something's missing in my life. Like a part of me has been cut off. Imagine waking up one day to realize that your legs were gone! That you left a world of freedom, where you could walk and jump and run, without even saying goodbye. That's how I felt. And that's how I still feel. Anyway, it's getting late now, Emy. You have to sleep. Thanks for talking to me. I feel a little better."

Nope. I felt a little worse. Still, I appreciated that she had listened. At least she hadn't laughed.

"Good night, Rosie!"

"Good night, Emy. I love you."

"I love you too!"

I listened to Emma's quiet breathing. I tried to match mine to hers, but hers was so much faster that it was impossible.

In my head, I started to compose this letter. Well, this story. Or whatever it is. I also thought about flying. And about Peter and Grace, who were and always will be completely real to me, even if I never see them again.

And Patrick. Oh, Patrick! The boy we saved from his father's nightmare! He was almost like a little brother to me. He was as real as my own sister. I had tried to stop thinking about possibly never seeing him again because it was too painful, but I found myself finally thinking about how much I miss him.

Would I never see him again? Or Peter and Grace and all my friends who sang in the Candy Cane Choir underneath the big rock, my favorite rock, that I loved to practice flying off?

How I would miss the Mysterious Lady with her long blonde hair and big eyes. Every time I went to the Garden of Roses, she was there. She'd sing the most beautiful opera song, the same one every time, as she danced around the flowers, her golden hair trailing behind her. I never had the chance to talk to her. I was always too shy. And now, will I ever get another chance?

But, Aunty, there is hope yet.

I am writing this because I want you to understand me,

Aunty, for very few people do, but I also hope that you may have a solution for me. A way to help me get back.

Aunty, I am starting to think of my dream world as the Lost Land of My Childhood. I don't want it to be that way. I want it to be the Found Land of Forevermore.

Please tell me you have a way to bring me back.

The Composition of Life

Karuna Chandran

The deity's fingers moved as swift as the wind as they carried him across the keyboard. His performances were always simply astonishing to all who watched him. The lovely sound of his instrument reverberated throughout the megaron. All eyes were focused on the wonderfully artistic Apollo as he played his melancholy piece on the piano. Little did they know how much the piece reflected his mood. While he may not have played a single note out of tune, he felt his movements to be much akin to a robot following a program mindlessly. The piece lacked depth and emotion, and he felt pained at being forced to spend his time on such a meaningless pursuit.

The problem had started decades ago. Gods and goddesses each had their own unique specialties. Apollo had several, like being the sun god and being in charge of raising and lowering the bright star every day. It seemed, every decade, he would simply discover another. He was pleased by this, of course. As an immortal, you had to keep yourself busy! But one dark year, his mother, the modest Leto, was in a dreadful musical mood. She longed to hear sounds more sophisticated than what her simple minstrels could produce. So, of course, she requested that Apollo try out the piano for her. And, of course, he was simply a genius at it. His soft fingers seemed to perfectly fit the smooth instrument. So his mother had him practice, day in and day out. She made him learn every single type of instrument she could get her hands on, from drums to bagpipes. He was harried for years. Soon, word got out in Olympus of his skills. Apollo had a feeling his sister, the cunning Artemis, might have had something to do with it. Not long after, he was proclaimed God of Music. But he had never wanted that. He felt no passion, like he did for the radiant sun. It was just meaningless sounds strung together in a random fashion. He could no longer conceal what he felt. He had to make it all stop.

So during his performance, he simply did stop. The crowd thought for a few moments that the silence was simply a part of Apollo's masterpiece. But eventually, they all blanched as they saw Apollo get up and walk out.

Apollo heard the cries of the crowd, astonished and angry as he flung the doors of the concert hall open. As he tried to make a swift exit, his sister Artemis stopped him.

"WHAT do you think you are doing?" Artemis demanded of him.

"I'm leaving. Can't you SEE that?" Apollo exclaimed. His sister always knew how to test his patience.

"I meant, how could you just walk out? You have a commitment to the world, to share your music and bring joy. Not only that, but do you really want Mother to find out what you have done?" Artemis asked.

"I certainly don't..." Apollo admitted. Anyone who thought that Leto was kind, gentle, and could never hurt a fly certainly did not have her as a mother!

"Then go back! Apologize to the crowd of people that you just left hanging, all because, like a pubescent mortal, you decided you were too good to handle your duties!"

"It's not just that, Artemis! I have never enjoyed music. Leto saying that music is my gift doesn't make me appreciate it any more. Isn't my happiness important too?"

"I guess… But do you really despise it so much that you are going to leave everything behind?"

"It's not just that! I can't deal with these expectations that everyone is pushing on me! Don't you think this is my decision to make? I've been alive a long time, Artemis. I think that it is time I started showing it," Apollo declared passionately.

Artemis sighed. "Do whatever you want Apollo. I just think that you haven't thought this through," she told him.

"Trust me, it's the only thing I have been thinking about,

for a long time," Apollo said.

Much, much later…

For a couple of years, Apollo lived alone in Pieria, far away from the world of Olympus. He still performed his godly duties, but stayed in the mansion he had for himself in complete isolation, other than a couple of hundred servants here and there to manage the place. It was a marvelous structure, in all its shining white glory. The large columns stretched up to the top of the building, until they reached the magnificent sprawling roof. But the real marvel was the giant statue of Apollo raising the sun. In its inviting warm colors, it immediately drew the eye. What made the whole place sorrowful though was that people seldom came to the gorgeous island. The mighty Zeus sometimes tried to compel Apollo to come back, calling him an irrational child, but nothing he could say would change Apollo's mind. Music just wasn't for everyone and until the world forgot about his "talent" for music, there he would remain.

One day, Apollo was watching one of the shrines someone had created of him. He had a portal room, allowing him to see and hear any location he chose. It pleased him to see mortals fawning over him. It made the bitter edge of loneliness almost go away. He watched as a boy slowly came up and started playing on his little ukulele. The sight of the instrument brought back painful memories, and he almost stopped watching the shrine, but then the sound of the instrument hit his ears. It was mind-bogglingly terrible. The cacophony sounded like harpies crying, and it made his ears almost bleed. He told himself that he must go down to Earth and stop that terrible excuse of a melody.

He appeared in regular day clothes with jeans and a T-shirt that said, "Apollo 11 was named after me." He stormed through, all the while cupping his delicate eardrums in his hands and spoke to the boy in a barely contained manner.

"Excuse me, but may I show you how to play that tune?" Apollo inquired as politely as he could under the circumstances.

"Absolutely, but, you know, I have been practicing this piece for a while, so you may need my help," said the boy.

"I'm sure you have," Apollo mumbled. He picked up the instrument. His fingers reached out to the ukulele almost instinctively and slowly moved across. It had been so long since he had touched an instrument, and he had to shift his body to let it rest comfortably under his arm. He felt his stomach in knots, a reaction to willingly holding something he had avoided for so long. But this boy HAD to be shown the right way to play, so he started to strum. In the beginning, he was a little shaky, but as the song went on, he felt his tensions ease as his body relaxed.

He could feel as much as hear the slight nuances of the song, the beautiful way four strings could be endlessly played in any pattern. He could hear his feet softly tap the pavement in response to the music that was softly vibrating through his fingers. The wood felt smooth under his long fingers. It truly was a magnificent instrument, and he appreciated the craftsmanship. As he played the piece, every now and then he missed a note, but he didn't care. He felt something he had never felt before when playing an instrument. Joy. The knowledge that he was doing this, not because he was forced, but because he wanted to sit down, relax, and soak in the caressing sounds made all the difference. He didn't care who was watching him or judging him. And this new realization carried him through the piece. And the next. And suddenly it had been hours of him and the instrument. Once it became evening, he slowly lowered the sun down, with a sense of closure to his movements. The boy watched him the whole time, rapt in his playing.

"Here you go, little child. I hope you have a good time

with this instrument. It's very special," said Apollo, handing the instrument over.

"I'm sure I will," said the boy as he smirked.

Wait. That smirk is so familiar... And he stared in incredulity as the boy slowly changed into someone else. Artemis, with guile written on her smug face.

"Well, that worked out a lot better than expected," said Artemis cheerfully.

"Artemis? I can't believe you tricked me like that!" said Apollo, stunned.

"I couldn't see you sulk any longer. It was just depressing! And by the way, that wasn't me forcing you to play out there for hours. That was all you!" said the goddess cheerfully.

As she sauntered away, Apollo knew he had to say something to her.

"Thank you, sister, for showing me the happiness that music can bring to me," said Apollo.

Artemis's features softened as she smiled back at her brother.

A Vision

Sabia Zakia Irfan

I flung myself onto my bed and slowly drifted into a well-deserved sleep. My consciousness was propelled through thick white clouds that smelled of cinnamon. I landed on a small sailboat in open waters, appointing myself captain. The sky was painted in vibrant hues of violet, red, and orange, in perfect harmony.

I felt at peace. Suddenly my ship was struck by violent torrents of wind. It knocked the cup of steaming cocoa that had magically appeared in my hand into the sea. The sky blackened with a dark storm, pouring sheets of thick, hot blood.

Each drop sprouted a revolting boil on my skin as the ocean warped into a whirlpool. Waves crashed and tossed my boat, heaving me overboard. I clawed the water with my frozen hands as it dragged me into its depths. My lungs screamed for air. I wrestled a final breath as I was swallowed whole.

Engulfed in nothingness, I emerged among hundreds of bleak tombstones implanted in the ground row by row—a graveyard. I was drawn to a peculiar ashen grave and crumbled to my knees in front of it. Engraved in neat black print were the words "*George Polar.*" My name! My gaze wandered to the date of my death: *July 31, 2020*. Tomorrow!

With no time to process, my soul was ejected from the cemetery in a beam of stars, returning me to my body. I awoke gasping and covered in sweat. Rays of the morning sun streamed through the window. I was going to die TODAY!

I needed to be prepared for *anything*. As quick as a bullet, I clambered out of bed, ignoring the blankets that tangled across my feet. I bolted and locked every single window and door. Dashing through the kitchen, I immediately grabbed the most lethal weapon closest in view and barricaded myself in my closet.

I camouflaged myself among my cashmere sweaters. I pulled my knees to my chest and rocked back and forth.

"It's okay… It's okay…" I repeated to myself.

Suddenly, powerful thumps echoed throughout my apartment. *Bang…Bang! BANG!*

"I know you're in there," called the stranger, hammering my door with his fists, trying to force his way in.

Should I open the door and risk assassination? I tightly squeezed my weapon, turning my hand white with numbness. I walked forward in a stiff zombielike trance.

"I have a dangerous weapon in my possession, and I am not afraid to use it," I declared.

I gripped it threateningly as my fingers skittishly unfastened the metal latch. I slowly opened the door. My head slumped between my shoulders; it was my brother.

"A...fork?" he said, confused.

"Y-yes," I affirmed, my face reddening.

"Took you long enough to open the door," he remarked, walking uninvited into my apartment. He snatched the fork from my hand. I was jolted back to reality with this comment.

"I'm going to tell you something that sounds crazy, but I need you to trust that what I'm saying *is* true. Can I tell you?" I said.

"Sure," he responded absentmindedly, viewing his reflection in my fork.

I roughly slammed the door and disclosed every detail of my vision.

"I think the spirits are giving me a warning," I proclaimed. "I read about this all the time in books."

My brother listened speechlessly till the very end.

"I need to make a call," he said bluntly after a long pause of awkward silence.

"For what?"

"For...weapons! *We* are going to need weapons!" he blurted. "I know a guy." He hastily left the room.

I pressed my ear against the wall to eavesdrop.

"Hi, Dr. Alzheimer? My brother is losing his mind. He thinks fairies and mermaids got inside his head and showed him a *vision* of his grave, where his death date is supposedly today."

Rage bubbled inside of me.

"Yeah, I'm disappointed that I didn't see the signs. Yes, I'll bring him by for a checkup right now. Bye." He hung up.

I calmly unlocked my door, then charged down the stairs and darted into the concrete jungle of New York. I was armed with nothing except my PJs, cell phone, and a watch strapped to my wrist.

Thunderous sounds of traffic boomed from the streets. Wild colors and bright lights danced on billboards, blinding my sight. I felt as if I was suffocating among the seas of people that crowded the sidewalks. I stumbled into lampposts and barely avoided falling into open manhole covers.

Suddenly, I stood face-to-face with a furry, little, black cat. Its eyes fixated on mine. It meowed innocently. This wretched feline's adorable act wouldn't fool me. I practically crashed through the glass doors of Starbucks, evading the creature's ominous aura.

The refreshing aroma of coffee wafted through my nose. I sat down, and I could feel the weight of everyone's gaze. A tall woman with a lemon-colored bob eyed me suspiciously as she *happened* to walk past me on her way to the restroom. A bulky gentleman in a blue-checkered shirt stuffed a gouda breakfast sandwich in his face as he *bizarrely* glanced at the empty seat next to mine. Finally, a wire-thin waitress in a brown apron *oddly* reached for the empty coffee cup on *my* table. That was the last straw! Every single person here was a potential murderer!

"Who wants a free blueberry muffin?" unexpectedly offered the cashier just as I was about to make my escape. I clutched my stomach as it growled. I hadn't eaten breakfast yet. It taunted me with its crisp brown color and ripe blueberries baked to perfection.

"I will," I answered without hesitation.

I reached the hardwood counter to receive the delicacy, but before I could seize it, the same beefy gentlemen clasped it with his meaty fingers. He shoved it inside his mouth, saliva dripping with each chew. He monstrously licked his lips with relish. That was MY muffin! Suddenly, his stomach began to gurgle and slosh. His face turned pea-green as he hurled the digested muffin and a pile of disgusting vomit onto the floor. He collapsed on a bystander, crushing him with his weight.

Food poisoning! This world was out to get me! I began to make my way toward the door.

"Excuse me," said a man in a deep voice.

My heart dropped into a petrified state. I turned to see a man with muscles the size of cannonballs. They were decorated with ghastly tattoos of skulls with tongues bulging from their mouths. He flashed a malicious smile. A shudder raced down my spine as he reached inside his sleeveless jacket. He was revealing a weapon!

I sprinted outside the shop to find that this criminal was following me!

"Wait!" he yelled as he hurried after me.

I ran from alley to alley until I managed to shake his trail. I crouched my scrawny body behind a garbage can. Police sirens blared through the city. They were most likely searching for that crook or me, thanks to my brother's notion that I was mentally unstable.

Soon the blazing sun was replaced with a starless night sky. The wind viciously slashed at my skin. I shivered in the cold. How long had it been? I quickly glanced at my watch—11:50 p.m. Ten more minutes until I had defied my future!

"I know you're here," a familiar voice menacingly said.

He found me! I had celebrated too soon, but I wasn't going to run. I needed to face him. I jumped from the trash bins and stood before him, glaring directly into his snakelike eyes.

"You listen here," I shouted in the most intimidating voice I could muster. I aggressively pointed my trembling finger at his chest. "You take a single step toward me, and I will...I will..." I couldn't find the words. "I will...call...*the*...police," I managed.

He probably could sense this was an empty threat. Nonetheless, it worked! The lump's sinister expression dissolved into shock. Fear was evident on his face.

"I just came to give you this back," he said in a quivering voice. He presented me with a black cell phone. I patted my pockets.

"You dropped it at Starbucks!" he sobbed.

My eyes widened. Who did I just threaten?

"Thanks for the phone," I said kindly, taking it from his sweaty hand. "Hey, don't worry, I won't call the police."

He sighed in relief.

"Why don't I walk you home?" I patted his back reassuringly.

"Okay," he sniffled.

I checked my watch; 11:57 p.m. Three more minutes!

As we exited the alley, honking noises filled our ears. A truck was heading for us at a vast speed, unable to slow down.

"Watch out," the Starbucks man bellowed as he dove out of the way.

Rooted in my tracks, the vehicle slammed into me.

Pain seared through my bones as I lay paralyzed. I gathered every ounce of my remaining strength and shifted my head in the direction of my watch. It read 11:59 p.m. As my eyes fluttered shut, I could feel my mind wander to the unknown—another vision.

I found myself back at the field of headstones. A man dressed in a green cleaner's uniform approached my grave. He placed a yellow bucket brimming with water at his side. He began to scrub the grimy rock with a sponge. I edged toward him. My heart shattered into pieces.

Glinting brightly in the sun were the words "*George Polare.*"

Today's Tomorrow Is Today

Kate Hwang

He sat on the third bench by the winding sidewalk that snaked through Baker Park. Earl often came here to revel in nostalgia. When he was a child, he used to play baseball games, climb trees, and hide under the playground equipment in the very same place. Today, he looked in the direction of the children and watched with a slight smile on his face. He could see a younger version of himself swinging on the monkey bars with the same ecstatic expression as the young child on the top bar wore today.

Sitting on the bench this warm Sunday afternoon, Earl suddenly felt an urge to join the youth and play like a child. The kids looked bewildered and frightened as he approached. They scattered in the opposite direction. Earl looked down at himself, his clothes ruffled in the wind that snuck through the holes and rips of his tattered shirt.

"Come back," he croaked, but they didn't look back.

He started climbing on the playground equipment, his gray face beginning to bead with specks of sweat. He went down the slide nine times that day, and every time he wondered why he was climbing back up and up and up again. He thought about it later, when he walked away from the park.

That night, Earl felt sick, unable to sleep properly. He lay in his small section of the sidewalk by the McDonald's tossing and turning. He was over fifty; he shouldn't be bothered by a few thoughtless kids?

He went back to the park the next day, like he'd done every other day. This time, it was deserted except for one small boy, sitting alone on the top of the slide. He climbed up and sat next to him, and to his surprise, the boy didn't avoid his presence by just sliding down.

"Hello," Earl said.

They casually shared a glance before he slid down again.

The boy looked at him with awe. On the slide beside Earl, he put on a look of courage and squeezed his eyes shut as he went down.

"Why didn't you run away from me?" Earl asked. He didn't seem frightened like the other children had been the day before. "All the other children did yesterday."

The boy shrugged while looking down.

"Let me tell you something," Earl said calmly. "Just because someone changes here..," he said while gesturing to his clothes and face, "it doesn't mean he's changed in here." Earl placed his hand on his heart. "I was a young boy once like you, and no one ran away from me then. I think people get scared when they see homeless people like I am now, but I'm no different just because of the way I look."

"Did you look like me when you were younger?" the young child asked.

Earl chuckled. "No, but, boy, remember what I said. Nothing compares to what's inside. We are bound to lose people if we only look on the outside." He chuckled again. "We all age and become wrinkly old men… But although I've had a lot more years than you, you are a lot stronger than me. A lot…braver…"

"How do you know that?" the little boy asked, beaming inside out.

"Because…it took me fifty-three years to go down that slide."

Earl looked out into the clear blue sky that shone brightly back at him. He went down the slide again and left the playground. He did not return to the third bench in Baker Park or the sidewalk by McDonald's. Today, he walked on past the duck pond with the cackling geese, past the row of newly furnished condominiums. He walked straight, then took a left, a right, then another left and stood in front of his mother's home.

The Blue Boy

Nora Ciak

Benny comes up to his mommy, tripping over his feet and clutching his stuffed bear. He tugs her apron for attention, only to be brushed away as she continues talking on the phone and washing dishes.

"Mommy," Benny says, looking up at her with wide hopeful blue eyes. "Can I play outside? Promise I'll be good."

His mother, too caught up in her conversation, just nods and shoos the four-year-old away. He cheers and stumbles excitedly toward the partially open back door and slips out.

Giggling to himself, Benny swings his bear around in the grass. The summer breeze ruffles his brown hair. The bubbling creek is crystal clear as it rushes over the rocks. He gasps when he sees a huge butterfly and unceremoniously drops his toy to catch it. He doesn't notice how close he is to the water, too caught up in trying to capture the butterfly. Suddenly, he hits his head on one of the sharp rocks and blacks out.

***

"Mom, I'm home!" Kate yells.

She takes her earbuds out, tosses her bag on the floor, and plops down on the couch with her legs hanging off the arm. After a few minutes of being on her phone, she looks up surprised that Benny hasn't come to ask her to play yet. Most days she would find it endearing to have her cute little brother excited to see her, telling her all about his day, talking a mile a minute.

"You're home early. Is there something wrong at work?" her mom says from the kitchen.

"Uh...wha—yeah, yeah. . .um, they, ah, they just let us out

early today." Kate shakes her head to clear her thoughts. "Um, do you know where Benny is? I don't see him around."

"He's not with you?" her mom asks, her voice tinged with worry. "I thought you were going to take him to see your boyfriend."

Benny loved hanging out with Steve, and Steve adored Benny.

"Steve was busy so he canceled last night," Kate says. Her troubled face mirrors her mother's.

The front door swings open as Emma skips in. "Hey Mom, I'm back from Sarah's party!" she cheerily says, toeing off her shoes. She freezes when she notices the panicked looks on their faces. "What's wrong?"

"Benny." That one word spoken breathlessly sent the three women running about the house looking for the youngest member of their family.

"Mom!" Kate yells, noticing that the back door was left ajar.

Heavy footsteps resound through the house as her sister and mom all but spring toward her. Her mom wastes no time in pushing the door open and running out onto the grassy hill scanning for any signs of her son while calling his name.

***

Benny wakes up to the sound of his name. Nervous calls and shouts.

"Why does Mommy sound so worried?" Benny questions, slowly getting up.

He notices that he is standing in the creek, but he can't remember how he got there. He furrows his eyebrows and tries to figure out what is going on.

"Benny!" his mother shrieks. She sounds closer than before.

"Mommy!" he answers. He tries to make his way up the

hill.

"Benny, where are you?"

"Benny, come here!"

"Benny!"

His sisters are calling for him. But can't they hear him? Maybe he isn't loud enough.

"I'm right here!" Benny yells, louder this time, tripping over his feet to get to his family.

He sees Mommy, Kate, and Emma turn from him, the sound of his father's old pickup truck dragging their attention away. Benny watches at a distance, his mommy running up to his father before breaking down in his arms. His sisters hold on to each other as Kate says something that only serves to make Mommy cry harder, shaking in Father's arms.

Benny slowly makes his way to the back of the house.

"Mommy, what's wrong? Don't be sad, Mommy." He hugs his mommy's leg, trying to offer some kind of comfort to stop the seemingly endless tears. His father murmurs reassuring words in her ear. The only phrase Benny can hear is "We'll find him, Rachel."

***

It is getting late. The sun has just dipped past the horizon. Benny plays with his bear as his family searches for someone. He looks up as they reach the crest of the hill, his father first, holding somebody, with his mommy and sisters a few paces behind, shoulders shaking as silent sobs rack their bodies. Benny runs up to his father, while trying to get a peek at the limp body that his father is cradling. A small wet boy with brown hair and cold blue skin.

***

A week passes, and the funeral and burial for Benny comes and goes. His father Henry is barely home, leaving before the sun is fully up and coming home late at night. Emma is with Sarah practically every day. Rachel takes it the worst, barely moving or talking. Kate is left picking up her mother's responsibilities. She only has a few days off before returning to her job. She needs the money for college.

After his family found the blue person, something seemed...off. Benny is confused. His parents stopped kissing him goodnight, and his father isn't around much. His mommy is visited by crying people who bring sweets and cards, Emma doesn't play with him anymore, and Kate barely has time for anything. He wonders why they pay less attention to him. After a week of no hugs or kisses, Benny can't hold back the confused, sad tears.

Rachel is downstairs when she hears it. Soft crying coming from above. It sounds exactly like...

"Benny!" she exclaims while running to the stairs.

There is another choked out sob; there is no mistaking that cry. It is Benny.

As Benny calms down, his crying turns to the occasional sniffle. He looks up as his mommy says, "Benny, don't cry. I love you so much."

He misses the way her face fell when she looked in the room. He runs up to her and hugs her skirt.

Rachel sinks to her knees crying. Benny isn't there. Benny is dead. He hit his head and drowned. He is gone.

Benny lets go of his mommy to retrieve his bear, so that she will cheer up. He plops it on her lap, gives her the biggest hug, and says, "Don't be sad, Mommy."

Rachel bites back a shriek as Benny's stuffed bear flies into her lap. She feels the ghost of a hug encase her. A whisper of Benny's voice telling her not to be sad.

***

That night at dinner, Rachel tells her family what happened to her earlier that day. The crying, the bear, the voice, and the feeling that Benny was there.

"Honey," Henry starts in a calm soothing voice. "Benny's gone. There's nothing we can do about that."

"No, no, he's not gone. I heard him. He was there."

"Emma, sweetie, why don't you head on up to bed?" Henry says, sensing where this is going and wanting to protect her from the conversation.

She gets up obediently and wishes everyone good night.

Once Henry is sure his daughter is out of earshot, he fixes his wife with a gentle glare. "Rachel, stop."

"You don't believe me," she says, eyes darting between her husband and her eldest.

"Mom, you're talking nonsense," Kate says.

"I know what I heard. It was—"

"Rachel, you were just missing him and thought you heard him," Henry says in a tone with finality. "We should all get some sleep."

***

This evening's conversation rings through Rachel's mind as she walks closer to the edge.

"Kate?" her father asked after Emma left.

"Yeah, I'll do the dishes," she responded, clearing off the plates before quietly muttering, "It's not like I haven't been doing it every day."

Rachel's watery eyes met hers. "What's that supposed to mean?"

"It means that ever since Benny died you haven't been doing anything. I've been driving Emma places, I've been cleaning, and I've been taking care of this family. Just because you miss him doesn't mean you get to just stop doing everything and dump all of it on me. That's not fair!"

"Kate, that's enough!" her father yelled.

"No, she needs to hear this!"

"You don't understand. He's still here," Rachel argued. She heard

Benny laugh, cry. She saw his toys scattered around the house. He. Wasn't. Gone.

"Mom, just stop. There's no one moving the toys, no one laughing or crying or whatever else you think you hear." Kate sounded broken and tired.

Rachel is falling, the wind whipping at her hair and tearing at her clothes. She doesn't remember anything after hitting the water, but suddenly she is in her house. She goes into Emma's room, kisses her forehead, and leaves a letter tucked under her pillow. She does the same thing to Kate, whispering a soft apology. She enters her room, stares lovingly at her husband for the last time, and softly presses her lips against his. She delicately places her letter on the pillow.

She walks into Benny's room and sees him sleeping peacefully on his bed. She gently shakes him awake.

"Mommy?" he blearily asks, a small fist coming up to rub the sleepiness out of his eyes.

She looks down at him, a little small smile gracing her lips. "Come on, Benny, we have to go."

She holds out a hand to him, then lifts him up on her hip. She holds him close as he clutches his bear and tries to stay awake. She walks out of the house for the last time, her smile turning sorrowful as she realizes all that she will miss. After saying one final goodbye, she leaves, walking down the street with her son on her hip, skin turning translucent in the moonlight.

About Lune Spark Books

Lune Spark Books aims to encourage children to engage in creating writing. We work with parents and young writers to promote creative fiction writing to help identify talent. We run annual competitions and creative writing classes and publish short stories by the young writers. For more details, visit us at http://lunespark.com/youngwriters/.

For the details of the contest or to enroll in the contest, please visit us at
http://lunespark.com/youngwriters/storycontest/.

Follow us on social media to keep up with the latest updates:

https://www.facebook.com/youngwriterscontest/
https://twitter.com/LuneSparkLLC

Other Anthologies by Lune Spark

A Window to Young Minds *(Age: 10+ years)*
This book is the first of the Lune Spark Short Story Contest's yearly anthologies and includes twenty-five award-winning short stories by young writers.

The Emotional Embodiment of Stars *(Age: 13+ years)*
Wonderfully wide-ranging, original, and enjoyable, this outstanding collection features twenty-seven short stories like *Mortimer*, in which an unwanted guest secretly follows a family through their heartbreaking sorrows.

Speaking Up for Each Other *(Age: 10+ years)*
Wonderfully wide-ranging, original, and enjoyable, this outstanding collection features twenty-four short stories like That Glowing Penny, in which a helpless girl has to live in fear of her own family.

Stained Glass Myths *(Age: 13+ years)*
A collection of twenty-eight award-winning stories by young adults. These stories encompass a wide range of genres, inviting readers to explore a wealth of important themes passionately crafted by these young writers—from a teenager going down memory lane after a tragic event at her school to a Jewish boy who writes letters to his older sister who's been taken to Auschwitz.

Just One More *(Age: 10+ years)*

A collection of twenty-nine award-winning short stories by middle grade children. These stories encompass a wide range of genres, inviting readers to explore a wealth of important themes passionately crafted by these young writers—from a beautiful dragon called Ephyral giving up her freedom to save her entire species to a fifteen-year-old girl named Louisa Brixham dealing with her brother being accused of a crime she committed.

Through Their Lenses *(Age: 10+ years)*

Through Their Lenses is a collection of twenty-nine award-winning short stories by tweens. These stories encompass a wide range of genres, inviting readers to explore a wealth of important themes passionately crafted by these young writers: from a girl going on a quest to release a curse bestowed on her by a witch to a guy trying to escape after being stranded in a different time.

www.ingramcontent.com/pod-product-compliance
Lightning Source LLC
Chambersburg PA
CBHW030756200726
48288CB00004B/1208

* 9 7 8 1 9 4 7 9 6 0 3 8 1 *